Terry Denton's

bumper book of holiday stuff to do!

Camping
City
Country
Boring? No!
Summer
Easter
Snow
Neighbourhood
Christmas
Beach

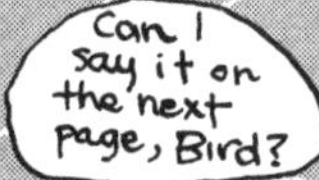

Terry Denton's
bumper book of holiday stuff to do!
Boring? No!
Summer
Country
Camping
City
Easter
Snow
Neighbourhood
Christmas
Beach
Go, Horse!

DEDICATED TO

Yenaj, Anivad,
and Aniram,
without whom
this book would
not be elbissop.

PUFFIN BOOKS

UK | USA | Canada | Ireland | Australia
India | New Zealand | South Africa | China

Penguin
Random House
Australia

Penguin Random House Australia is part of the Penguin Random House group of companies
whose addresses can be found at global.penguinrandomhouse.com.

First published by Penguin Books in 2012
This edition published by Puffin Books, an imprint of Penguin Random House Australia Pty Ltd, in 2022

Design by Marina Messiha and Terry Denton
Printed and bound in Australia by Griffin Press, part of Ovato, an accredited ISO AS/NZS 14001 Environmental Management Systems printer

A catalogue record for this book is available from the National Library of Australia

ISBN 978 0 14 377780 9 (Paperback)

Penguin Random House Australia uses papers that are natural and recyclable products, made from wood grown in sustainable forests. The logging and manufacture processes are expected to conform to the environmental regulations of the country of origin.

penguin.com.au

This is a book about ideas and expressing them in drawings and words.

You will need stuff.

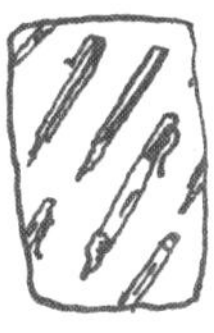

PENS IDEAS SENSES TIME

And a will to have fun . . .

IT'S YOUR SCHOOL CONCERT!
Can you find all these things in this picture?
THINGS TO FIND:
Superman •
Pharaoh •
Palm tree •
Avocado child •
Which way are we going?
I don't know.
Knee-deep.
Flob-bob.

Child in prawn costume • Boy caught by curtain • Darth Vader • Wolf • Sleeping audience member • Frog children • Girl with TV • Crocodile • Cat dreaming of fish • A real frog • Hungry caterpillar • Knight in armour • Yoda • Big banana • Woman reading newspaper • Giraffe • Dolphins • Penguin chorus • A big bird • Elephant • T–rex • The moon •

YOU ARE THE OCTOPUS

IN THE SCHOOL PLAY

What do you look like in your costume?

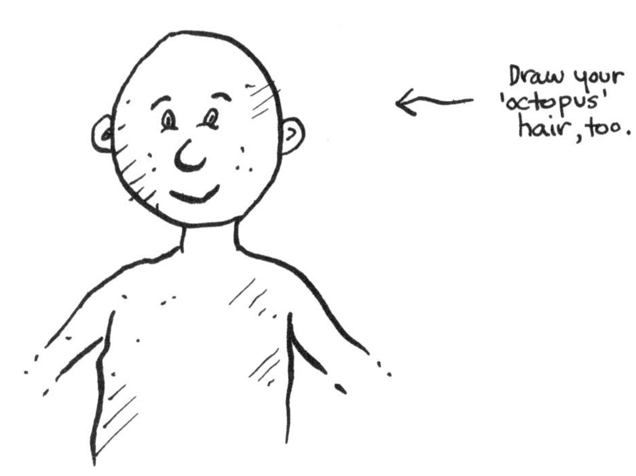
Draw your
'octopus'
hair, too.

YOUR BEST FRIEND IS A DRAGON

YOUR TEACHER IS THE BIG BAD WOLF

Add the heads to these people's costumes and colour in the one you want to be

WHO IS IN THE SPOTLIGHT?

Draw them

DRAW EXPRESSIONS ON THE AUDIENCE'S FACES
Great show!
YAY!
I'm stuck in the

Giraffe
Mum, there's a giraffe behind me.
CLAW
45

DRAW YOUR FOUR FAVOURITE TEACHERS

DRAW YOUR FOUR FAVOURITE FRIENDS

IT'S HOLIDAY TIME!

Write out your holiday to-do list

1. ....
2. ....
3. ....
4. ....
5. ....
6. ....
7. ....
8. ....
9. ....
10. ....
11. ....
12. ....

OKAY...

Now write out your holiday to-don't list

1. ....
2. ....
3. ....
4. ....
5. ....
6. ....
7. ....
8. ....
9. ....
10. ....
11. ....
12. ....

CHRISTMAS!
Find these things!
THINGS TO FIND:
A rabbit •
Santa asleep •
A llama •
Pelican •
Polar bear •
Joy to the World!
Perfume. Not more perfume!
It's mine. It's mine mine
Yum!
Not SOCKS again!!
He gave her pearls; she wanted a motor bike.
It's mine
It's mine
mine
mine.
Santa?
TOYS
The hippo broke my car.
No present for the cat. Humans get stuff. Cat gets nothing!
STUPID CAT
Happy Christmas, Bird.
Wow! A present for me?
A pair of socks?!
Yup!
!

Angry cat • Rhinoceros • Girl eating fish • Man chewing 32 times • Boy with broken car • Grandma asleep • Parents arguing • Hippopotamus • Girl with iPad • Child blowing up wall • Talking parrot • Boy sawing a hole • Man who hates socks • Girl with inflatable pool • Boy with baseball bat • Moose • Angel girl • Mice annoying cat • Woman who hates perfume • Old men fighting over gift • Hammer •

WHAT CHRISTMAS MEANS TO BIRD AND HORSE

DRAW WHAT
CHRISTMAS
MEANS TO
YOU

DECORATE
THE CHRISTMAS
TREE

And the cat!

WRITE A LETTER TO SANTA

(Tell him how very, very, very, very, very, very, very, very, very, very good you have been. And tell him what presents you would like.)

Dear Santa,

....

....

....

....

....

....

....

....

....

Yours..............................

....

WRITE A LETTER OF COMPLAINT TO SANTA

State clearly what you wanted and what you got and why you are NOT happy.

Dear Santa,

....

....

....

....

....

....

....

....

....

Yours ....

....

WHERE TO HIDE GIFTS

YOU ADD SOME MORE.

YOU TRY MORE.

Bird drew this one ↑
(I think Bird hates cats.)

TRUE/FALSE
What would you leave out for SANTA?

True ☐ False ☐

True ☐ False ☐

True ☐ False ☐

True ☐ False ☐

True ☐ False ☐

True ☐ False ☐

True ☐ False ☐

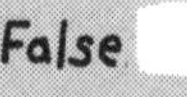

True ☐ False ☐

True ☐ False ☐

What would you leave out for his REINDEERS?

True False

True False

True False

True False

True False

True False

True False

True False

True False

BUILD YOUR OWN LANDING PLATFORM FOR SANTA AND HIS REINDEERS

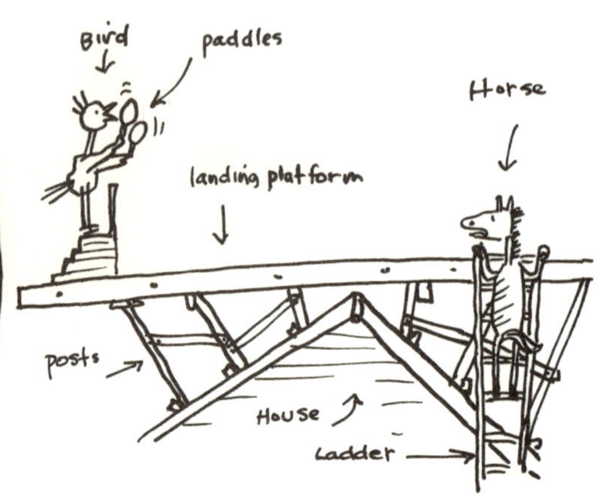

HOW BIRD WAKES HORSE ON CHRISTMAS MORNING

HOW YOU COULD WAKE YOUR PARENTS (Try six different ways)

WHAT'S INSIDE EACH PRESENT?

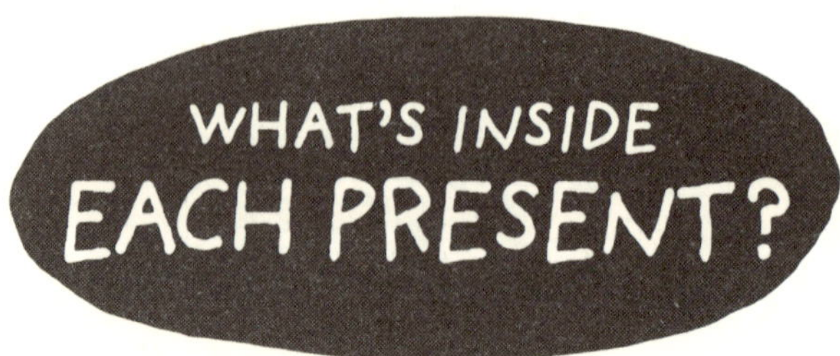

Write the matching letter next to the number below.

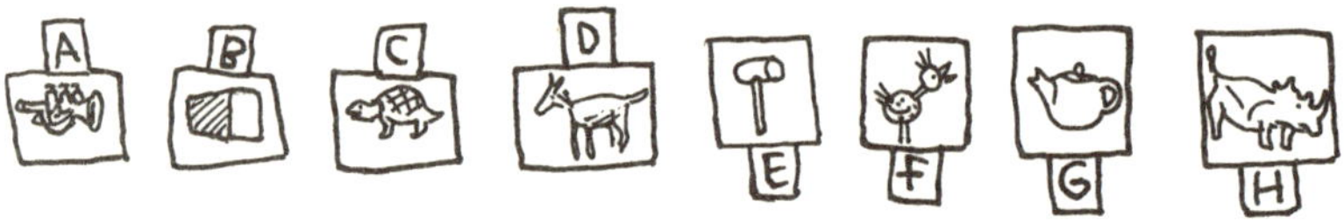

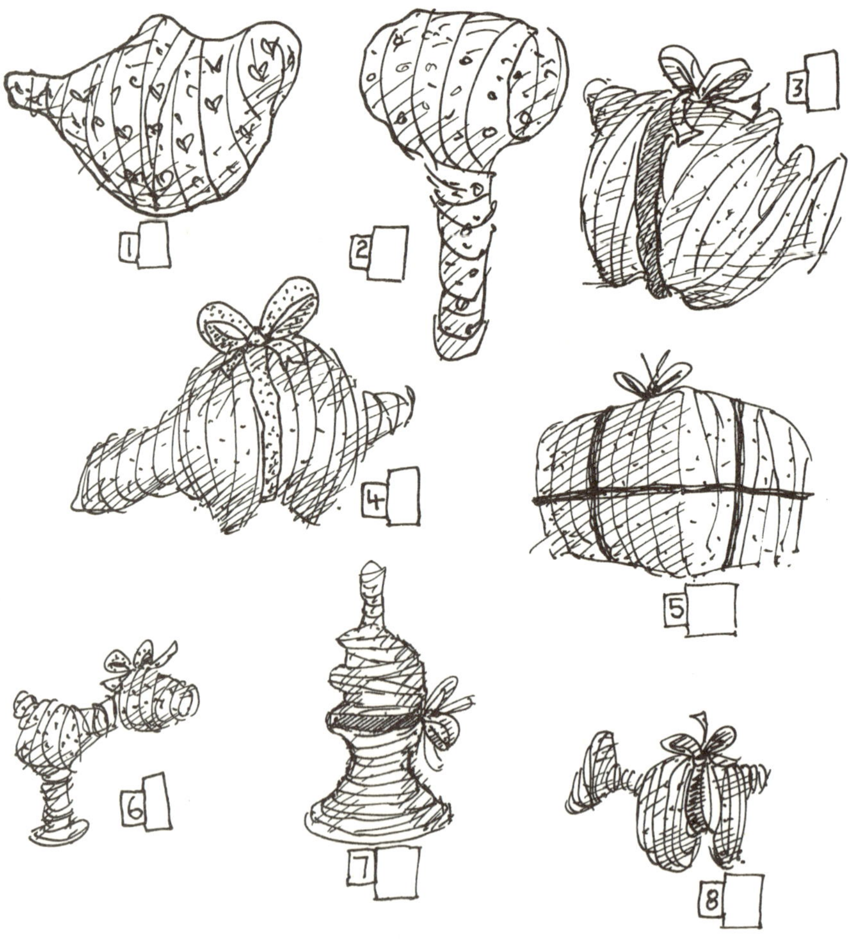

Write the matching letter next to the number below.

WHAT BIRD WANTED FOR CHRISTMAS

WHAT BIRD ACTUALLY GOT FOR CHRISTMAS

WHAT YOU WOULD LOVE TO GET FOR CHRISTMAS

WHAT YOU ACTUALLY GOT

BIRD has drawn HER RELATIVES and their faults

BIRD-BRAINED

LOUD

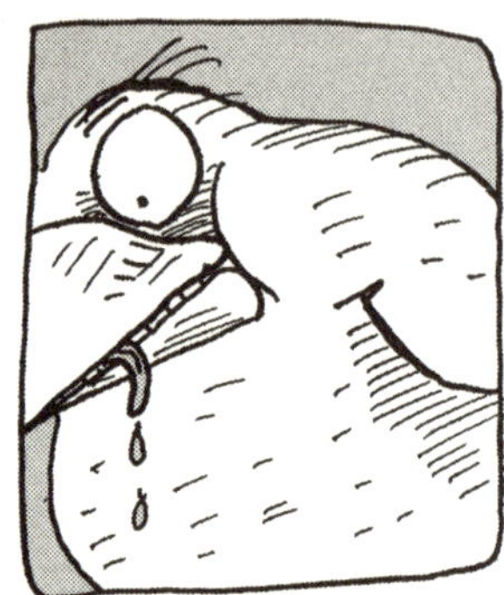

GREEDY

STEALS STUFF

SMELLY

MEAN

SARCASTIC

EASILY ANGERED

TOO FEARFUL

DRAW
some of YOUR
RELATIVES

DRAW YOUR FAVOURITE CHRISTMAS FOOD

DRAW SOME WEIRD
CHRISTMAS FOOD

CHRISTMAS QUIZ

1. What day is Christmas Day? ☐
2. What is Santa's surname? ☐
3. What is Santa's middle name? ☐
4. How many elves help Santa? ☐
5. What are their names? ☐
6. How many presents do they make? ☐
7. Where does Santa get his reindeers? ☐
8. What does he feed them? ☐
9. Which reindeer has a red nose? ☐
10. Why is his nose red? ☐
11. How does Rudolph guide the sleigh? ☐
12. How many houses does Santa visit? ☐

A. He caught it in his pencil sharpener.

B. 27

C. He buys them over the internet.

D. He's so old he's forgotten.

E. Rudolph

F. Reindeer food, of course.

G. GPS

H. He's so old he's forgotten.

I. Claus

J. 25th of December

K. 1,000,000,000,000,000,000,000

L. They're all called Otto, even the girls.

Answers: 1-J, 2-I, 3-D, 4-B, 5-L, 6-K, 7-C, 8-F, 9-E, 10-A, 11-G, 12-H.

BEACH HOLIDAY
Find all the things hidden in this picture
THINGS TO FIND:
Helicopter •
Sea eagle •
Fishing boat •
Hippopotamus •
Moose towel rack •
OUCH!
Yeah! Let's all hang our wet towels on the moose.

Beach volleyball • Mountain lookout • Polar bear on ice • Buried father • Boy with kite • Cricketers • Llama swimming • Girl getting shoulder ride • Bike rider • Polar bears sunbaking • Men playing bocce • Rhinoceros • Lady taking photo • Life guards • Cat fish • Meat pie-shaped rock • Kids building sandcastle • Giant crab • Family digging hole • Wombat •

YOU ARE GOING ON A BEACH HOLIDAY

What do you imagine your beach house will look like?

Things you would like to have in the beach house

1.
2.
3.
4.
5.

Things that you wish were NOT in the beach house

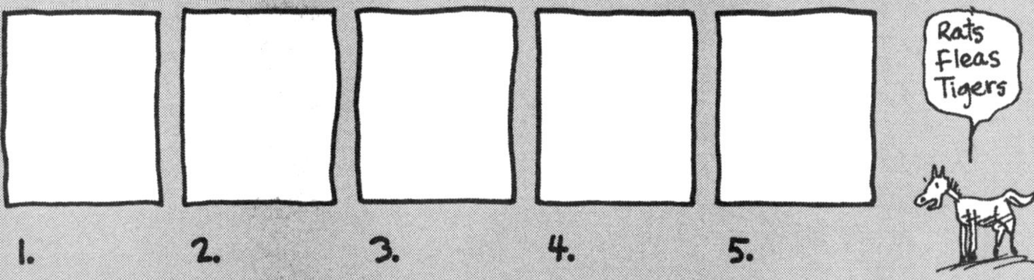

1. 2. 3. 4. 5.

DRAW MORE PEOPLE
AT THIS BEACH
(Then colour it in)
Swimming, diving, in boats, playing, burying each other, running, jumping, fishing, etc.

I'm a sea-horse.
Hat
So am I.
Mummy! A giant seagull!
Do you have any chips?

STUFF BIRD MUST TAKE TO THE BEACH

YOU

FISH SPOTTING

Look in the water and draw the fish you see

Flat fish

Three-eyed Puffer fish

Stingray

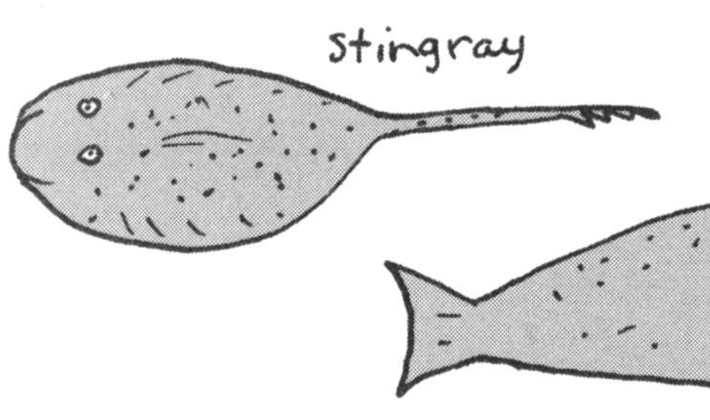

Small non-man-eating shark

Very Ugly fish

(Horse imagined this after accidentally swallowing a jelly fish.)

YOU

But . . . if you can't see fish . . . then MAKE THEM UP

DRAW AN UNDERSEA WORLD

It may be real or imagined

school of little fish, sharks, whale, eels, turtles, jelly fish, long fish, bubbles,

alien space craft, elephant, giraffe, toad fish, puffer fish, h, starfish, seahorse, rocks, coral, weed, stingrays, diver,

school of little fish, sharks, whale, eels, turtles, jelly fish, long fish, bubbles,

clams, small clams, giraffe in diving suit, shipwreck, squid,

THINGS YOU MIGHT SEE AT THE BEACH
True or False?

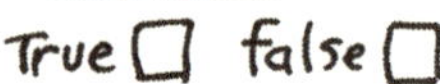

True ☐ False ☐

True ☐ False ☐

True ☐ False ☐

True ☐ false ☐

True ☐ false ☐

True ☐ False ☐

True ☐ False ☐

True
false
True
False
True
False
True
false
True
False
True
False
True
false
True
False
True
False
True
False
True
False
True
False

THINGS I LIKE OR HATE ABOUT THE BEACH

LIKE HATE

LIKE HATE

LIKE HATE

LIKE HATE

LIKE HATE

LIKE HATE

LIKE HATE

LIKE HATE

LIKE HATE

LIKE HATE

LIKE HATE

LIKE HATE

LIKE HATE

LIKE HATE

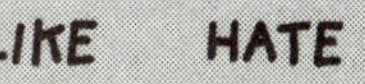

LIKE HATE

IT'S SANDCASTLE drawing time

Bird and Horse did this

Bird

Bird-brain.

I did the best bits.

OHRSE horse

Be Sun smart.

Bird is standing on nothing!!

Orange

Try colouring this page.

NOW **YOU** DRAW
A SANDCASTLE
(with lots of seaweed,
towers, shells
and flags)

DRAW A MASK, SNORKEL AND FINS ON THE DIVERS

Draw more people, fish and turtles.

DRAW A SEA MONSTER

Make it big, ugly, scary and a bit fluffy

Argh!

DRAW THE PIRATE'S TREASURE

YOU GO
DANCING
WITH A SHARK
Watch out you don't become dinner, Bird!

YOU JUST BOUGHT **CHIPS** AND THE **SEAGULLS** ARRIVED. DRAW LOTS OF SEAGULLS

Are they thin or thick?

I'm on a diet.
Did you say: CHIPS?
Quiet, Horse. They haven't seen us.

DRAW THE THINGS BURIED IN THE SAND
Can you dig me out now, Bird?
Hmmm. Maybe.
Unfair! They buried me while I was asleep

Caw! caw!

WHAT'S IN THE BIG GROPER'S STOMACH?
A couch?
A fridge?
A Gorilla?
A dragon?

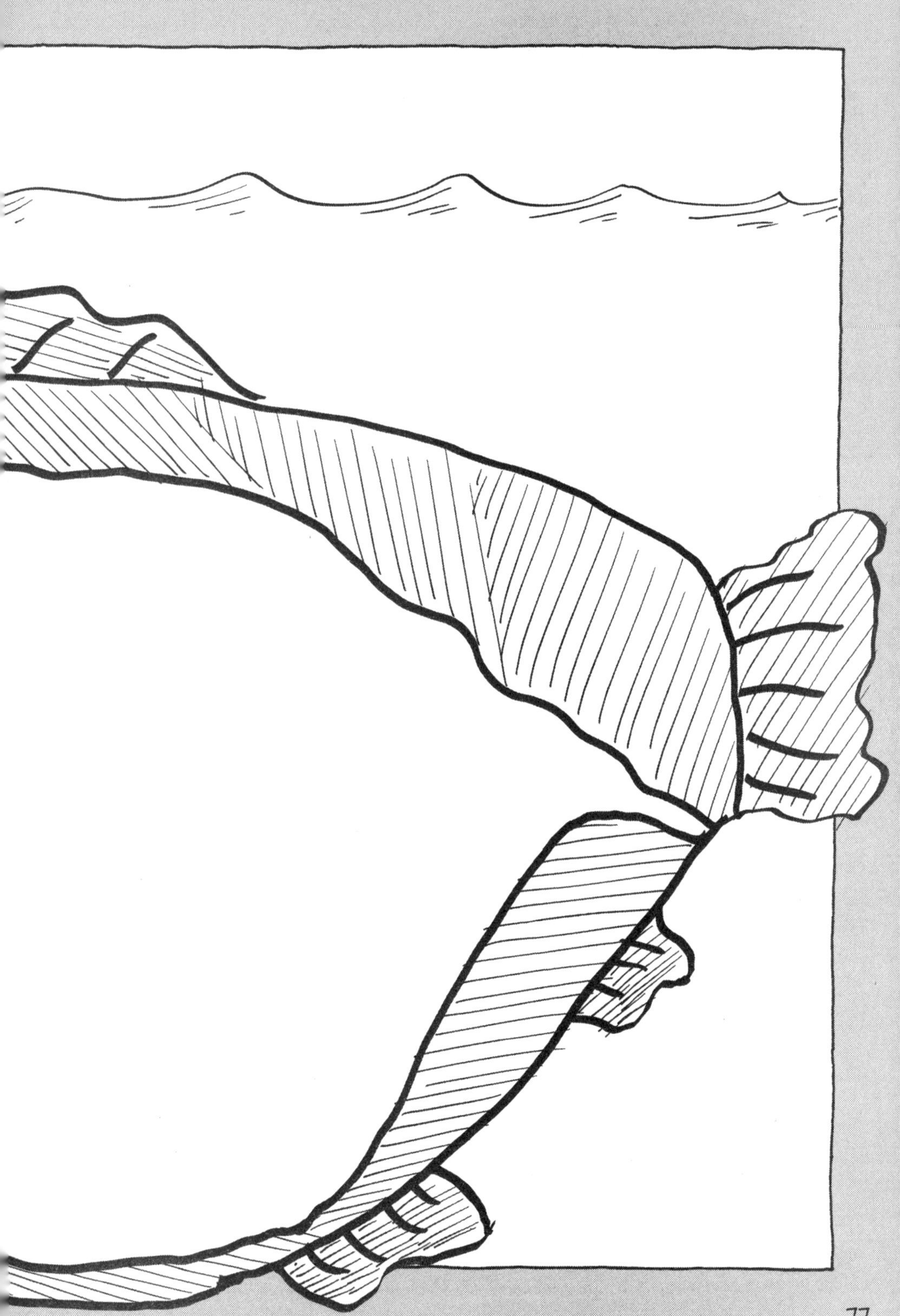

CITY HOLIDAY
Find the . . .
THINGS TO FIND:
Very wet building •
Car accident •
Fried egg •
Giraffes •
Big crab •
MARINA inc
Help!!
Hi.

Rhinoceros • Bird and Horse statue • Pineapple • Someone falling (almost) • Large finger • Giant bird • Building that looks like a large hairy pickle • Peanut • Swimming pool with sharks • Lost elephant • King Kong shopping • Crane • Big pumpkin • Stretch limo • Flying fish • Flying bird • Hamburger car • Birthday cake • Fast elevator • Runaway dumplings •

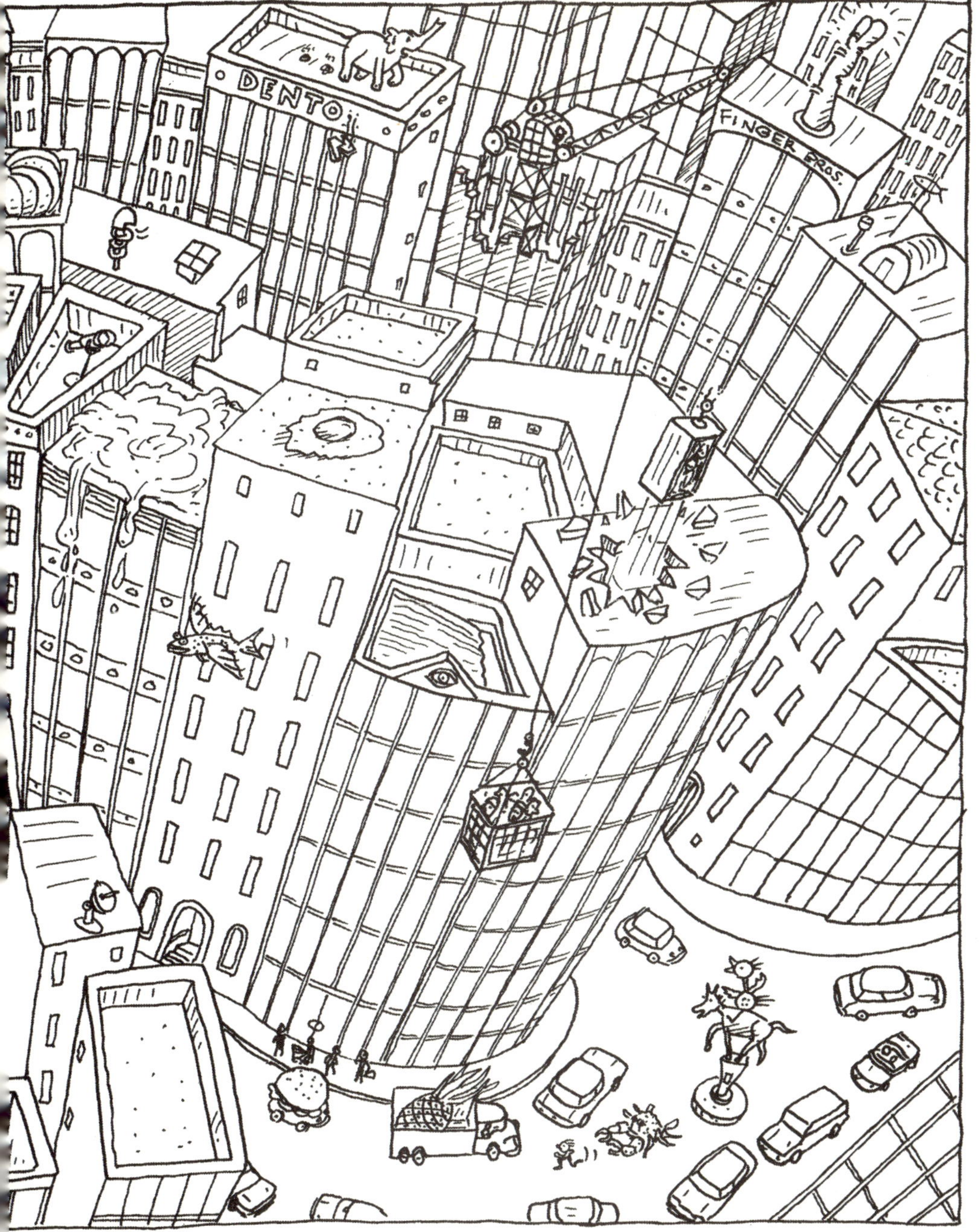

First I draw a horizon line. Then a dot low down on the page. This dot is the spot from which everything comes.

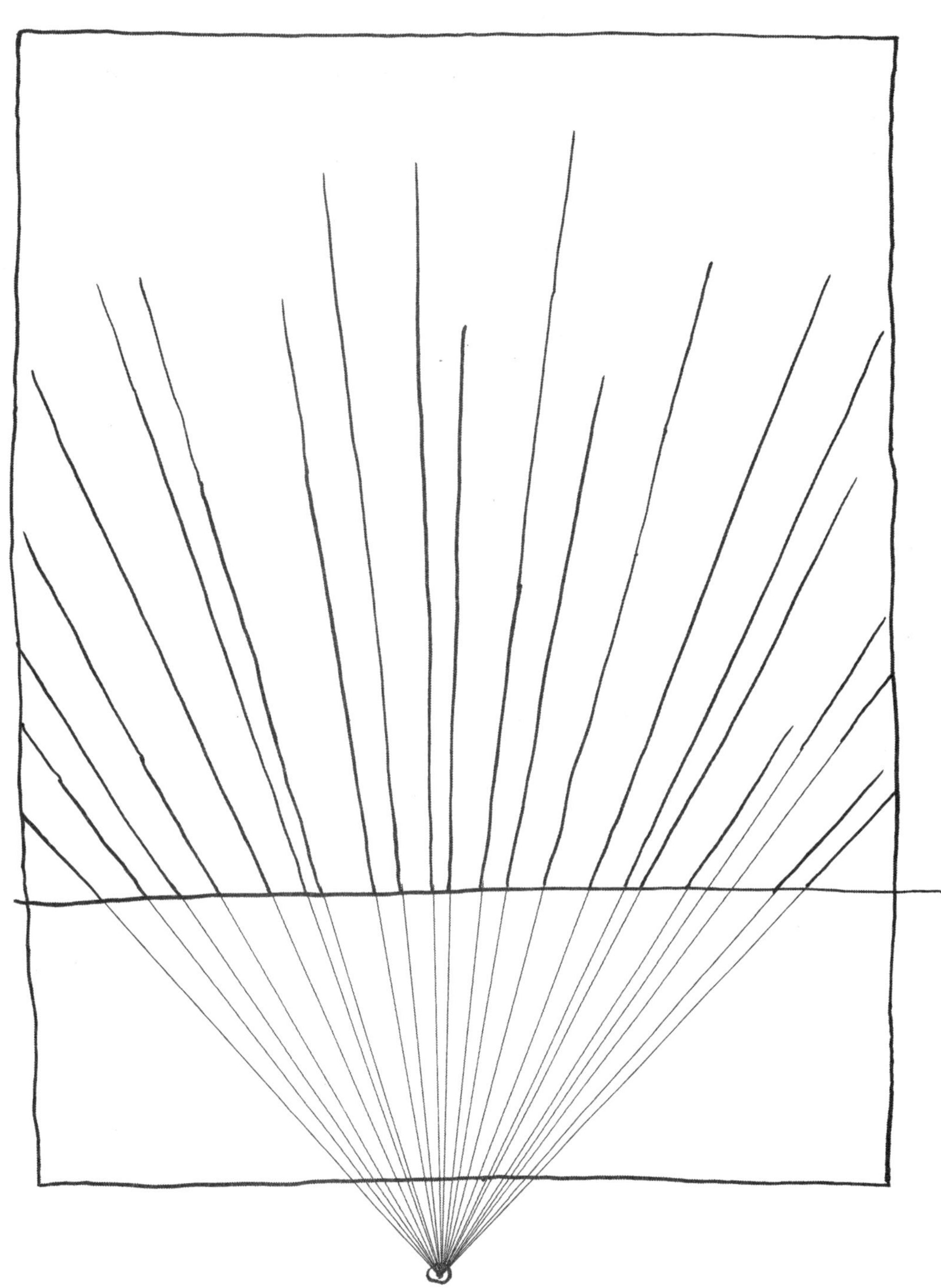

Now I draw lines coming out from that dot. You could even use a ruler for this. I call these radiating lines, like the sun's rays. They make the 3D effect.

MORE PERSPECTIVE

Then I throw away the ruler and I draw rectangles. Their corners fall on those radiating lines. You could put some thin paper over this page and trace my drawing just to get the idea.

Now I give the building all the details, like windows.
I've left you a few to finish.

NOW YOU TRY THE PERSPECTIVE.

Start with the horizon line, then a dot, then the radiating lines.

Okay, now try it again. This is not an easy drawing, so you won't get it looking good the first time. Just keep practising.

MORE
PERSPECTIVE

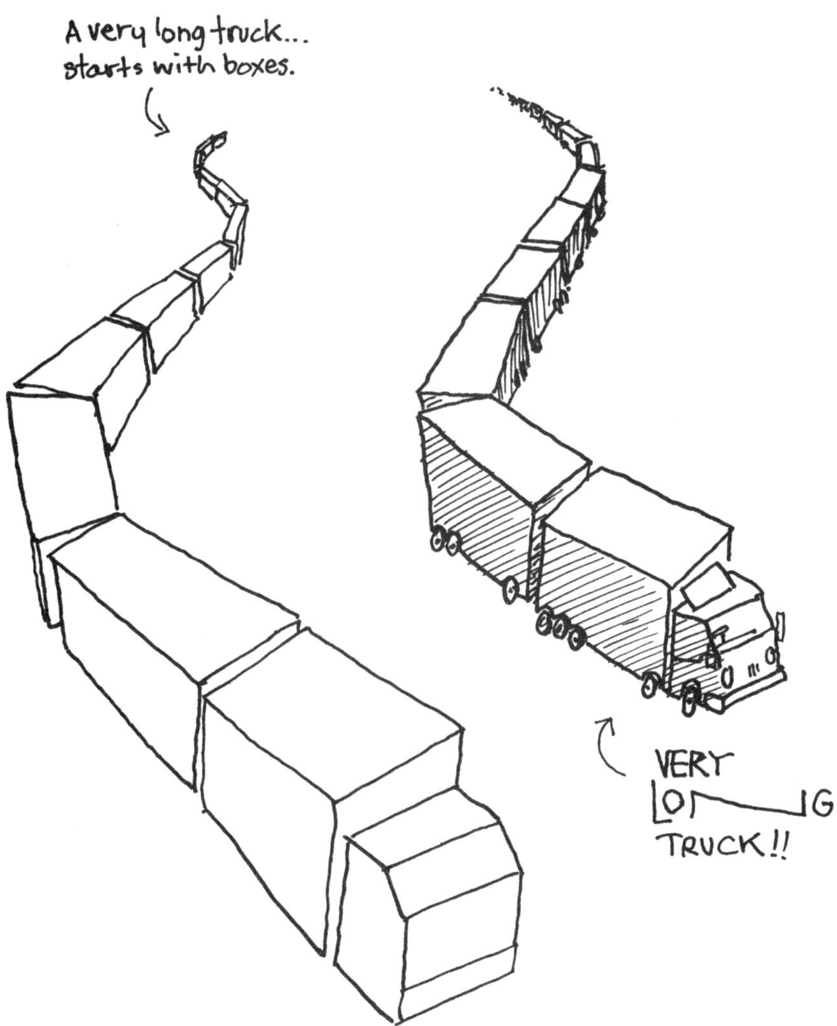
A very long truck...
starts with boxes.
VERY
LO——G
TRUCK!!

oink!

Find the KID
without a mobile
phone

YOU ARE LOST IN THE SHOPPING CENTRE IN THE CITY. Find your way to the car.

$$$$$$
CAKES
DRINKS
JEWELLERY
CAKES
B
NO!
COFFEE
MYSTERIOUS SHOP
Where's Willy?

OTHER COOL TYPES OF TRANSPORT

No car . . . No bus . . . No tram

YOU DRAW SOME

YOU ARE ON A ROLLERCOASTER
Draw the expressions of the people who are riding with you

FEED THE CUTE PIGEONS IN THE PARK
GIMME!

ADD MORE CARS TO THIS TRAFFIC JAM
PENCILS
GLOBAL FISH ENTERPRISES

FI SH
That means you!
DO NOT GO BEYOND THE FRAME OF THE PICTURE
More FISH
GIRAFFE DELIVERIES inc.
S
GHOTI
Yeeha!

FIND THE DANGEROUS KILLER DUMPLING

THINGS YOU LIKE AND HATE ABOUT SHOPPING

I hate shopping!
I love shopping!
HATE
HATE
HATE
HATE
HATE

DRAW
people looking out
the windows

DRAW

people in the elevator (they are watching the barking dog)

CAMPING
Can you find ALL these things?
THINGS TO FIND:
Sinking car •
Rhinoceros •
Penguins •
Man fishing •
Giant squid •
Argh!
STOP!
N.Y.

Wombat • Rubbish truck • Big crab • Giant frog • Pelican • Llama up a tree • Man doing dishes • Hippopotamus • Mosquito • Quicksand • Kangaroo with joey in pouch • Canoeist • Holidaying pirates • Woman fishing • Man in hammock • Polar bears on holiday • Ants • Woman with head through tent • Kids playing ball • Toilet block • Ride-on mower •

SPOT THESE THINGS ON YOUR DRIVE TO YOUR CAMPSITE

FIND THINGS
THAT START WITH EACH LETTER

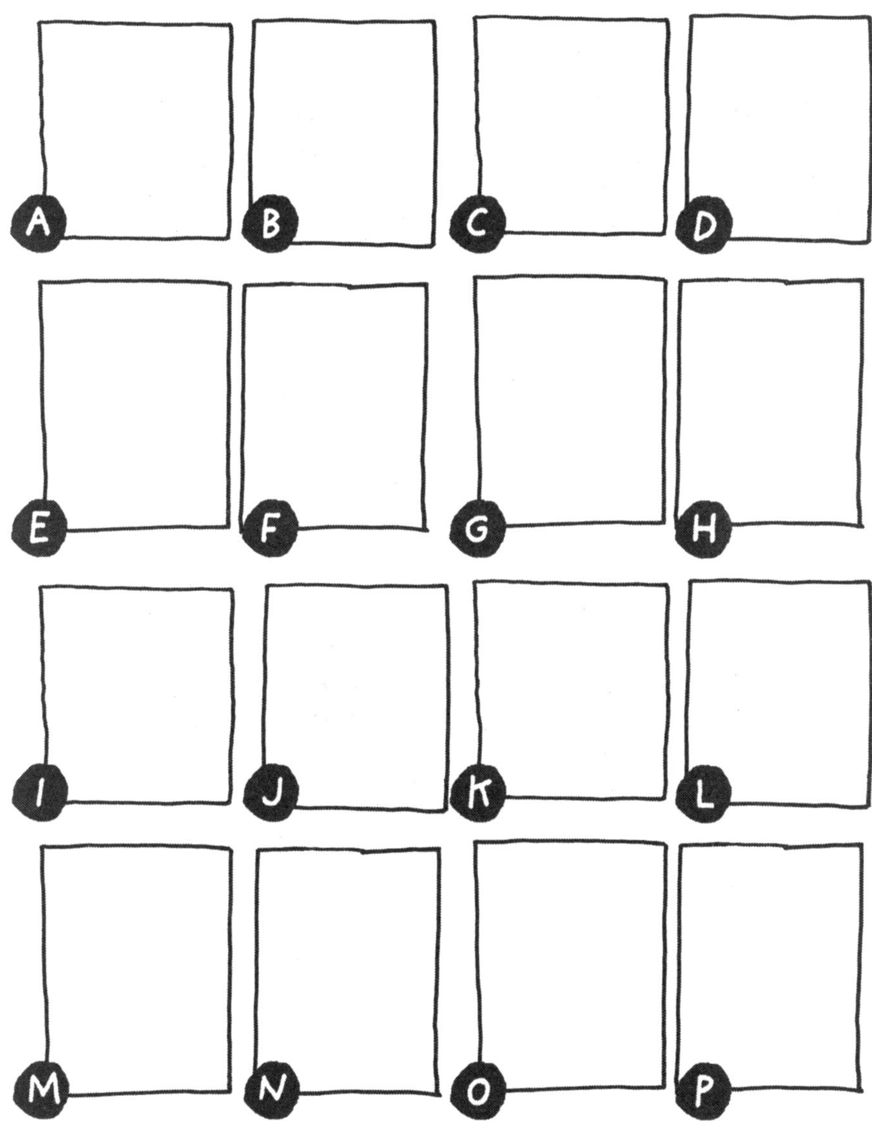

DRAW PEOPLE IN THE CANOE

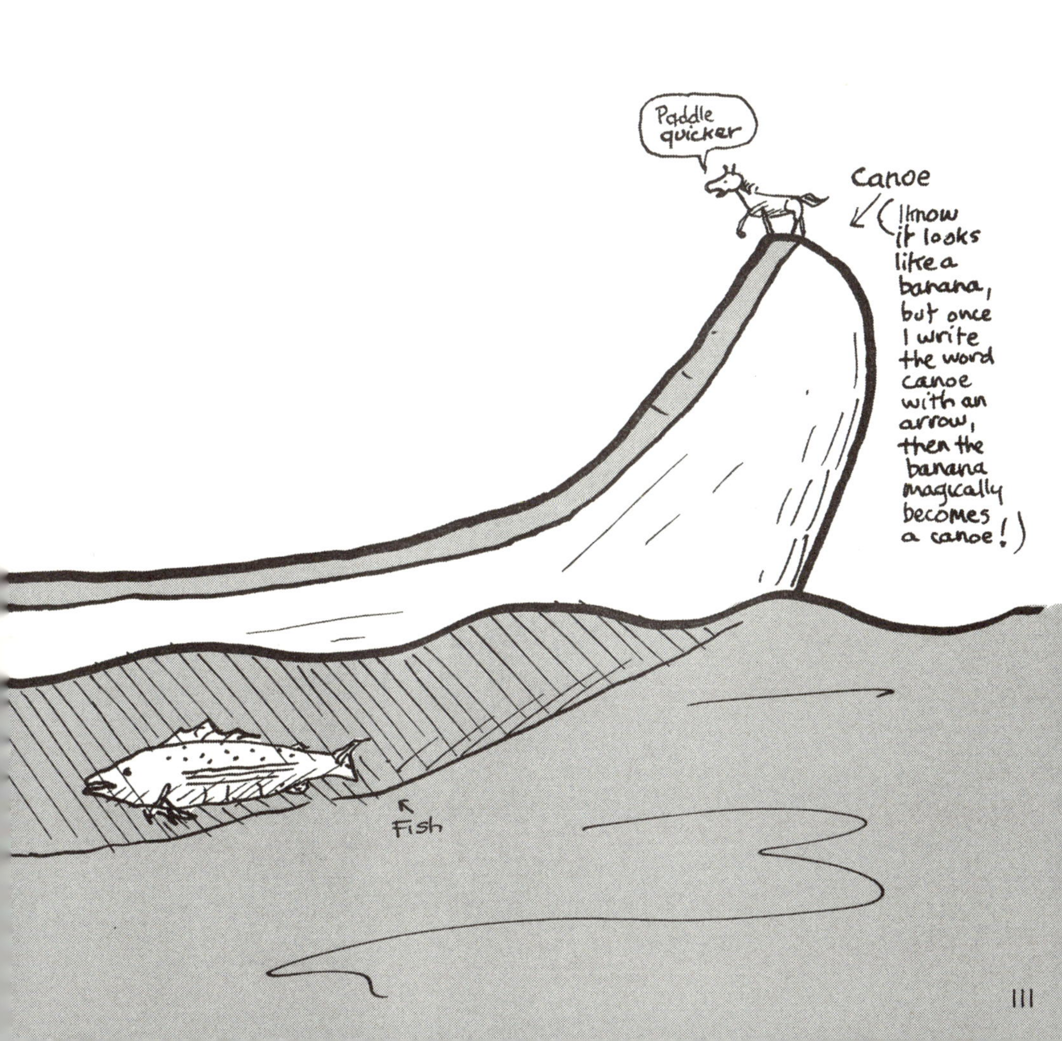
Paddle quicker
Canoe
(I know it looks like a banana, but once I write the word canoe with an arrow, then the banana magically becomes a canoe!)
Fish

HANG-GLIDING

Draw people on their gliders

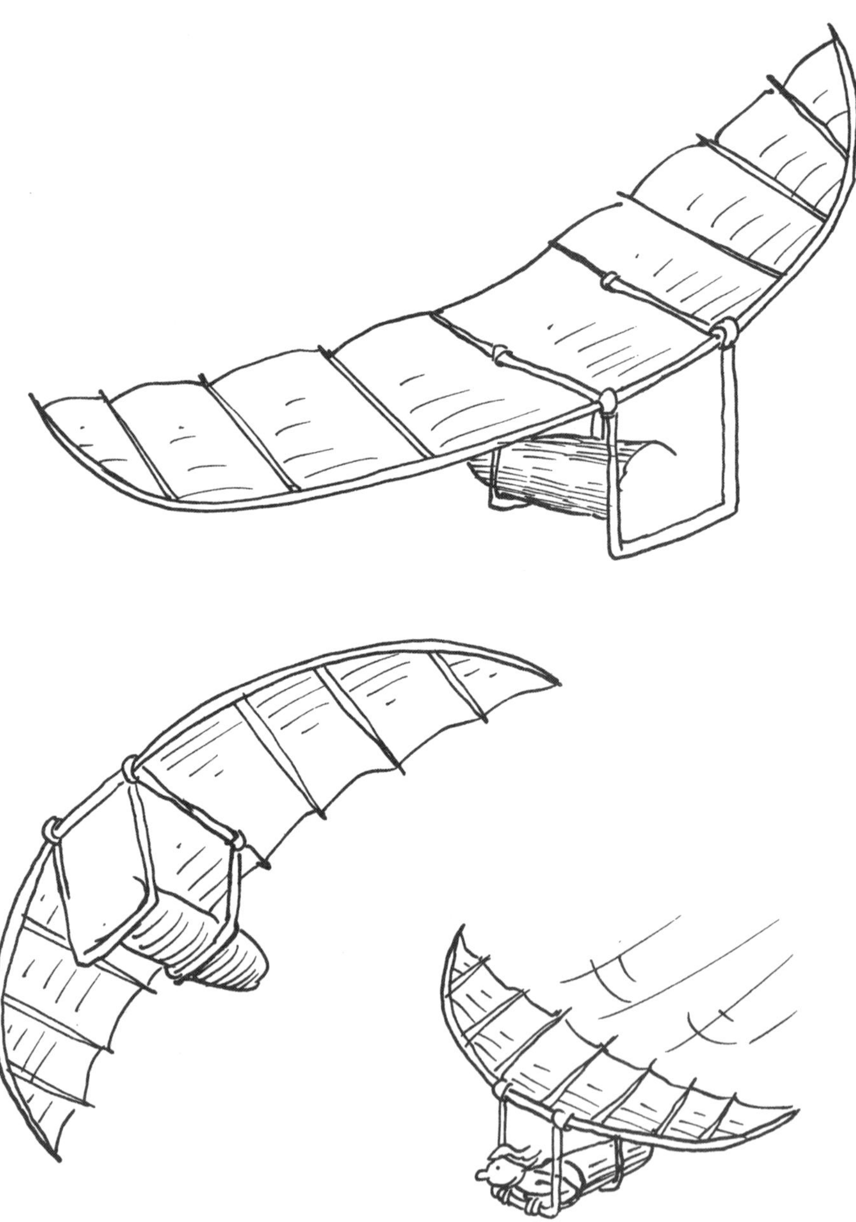

DRAW KOALAS
IN THE TREES
I am a treehorse! What ever that is.

DRAW THE BOAT PULLING THE SKIER

DRAW THE REFLECTIONS IN THE WATER

SWISS ARMY KNIFE MAKE YOUR OWN

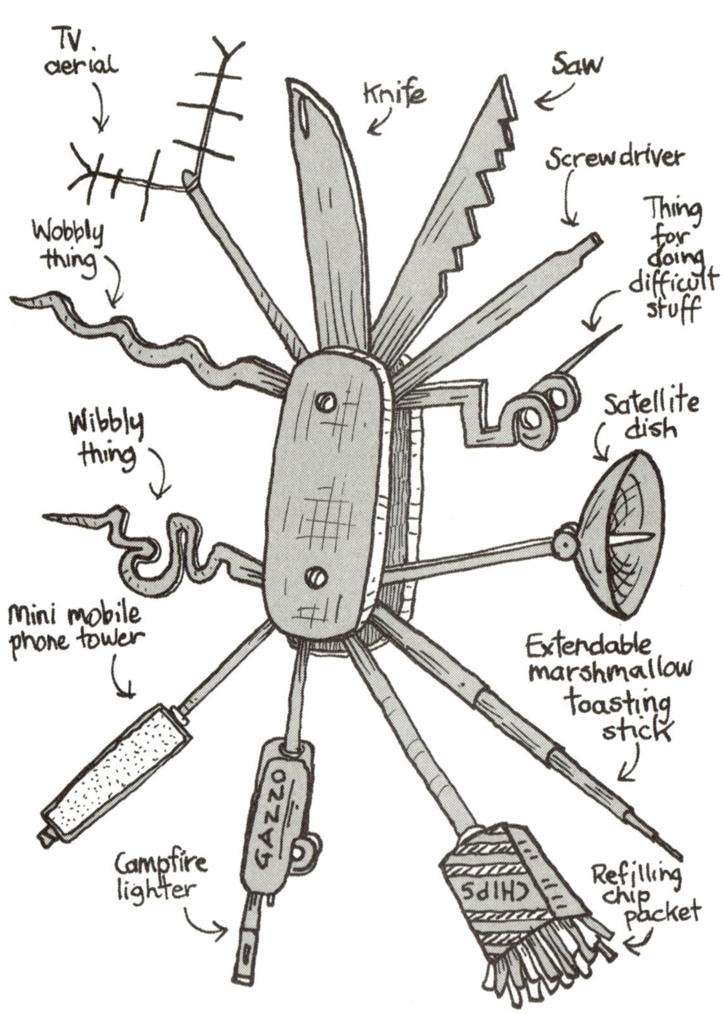

ME

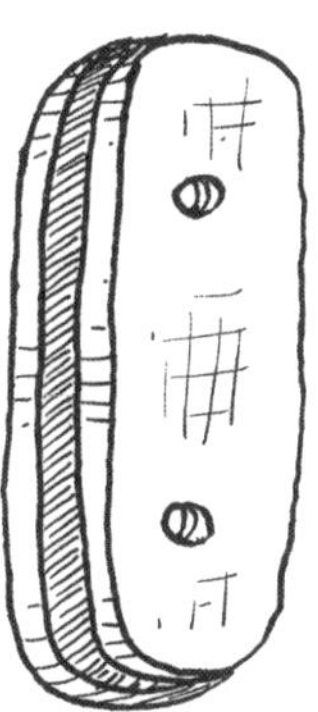

YOU

WHAT IS IN THE CAMP STEW?

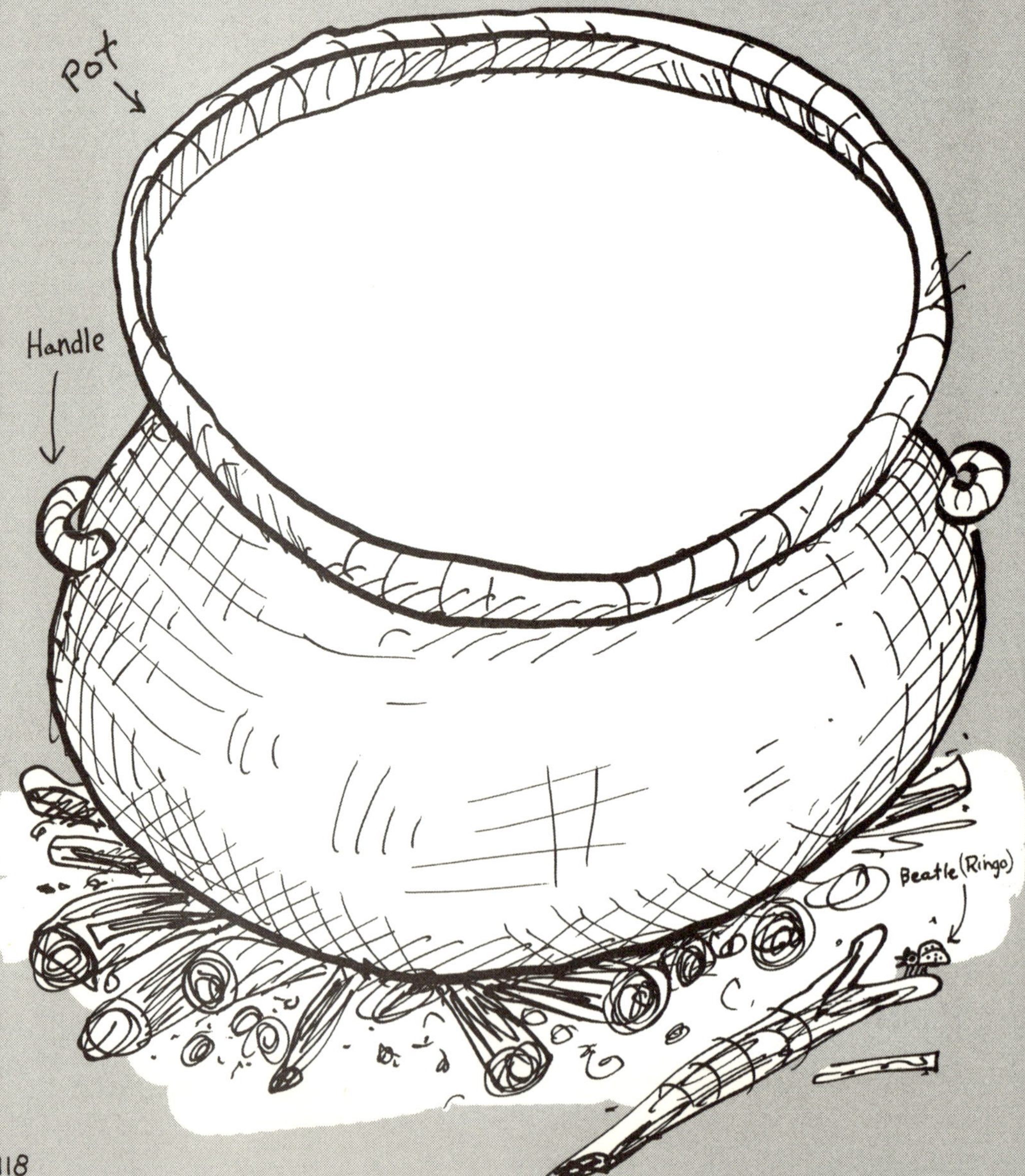

FILL UP ALL THE PICNIC DISHES
CHOCOLATE

YOU HEAR
NOISES AT NIGHT
Write down what the
noises are and draw
what you think
made them
HOWL!
HOWL!

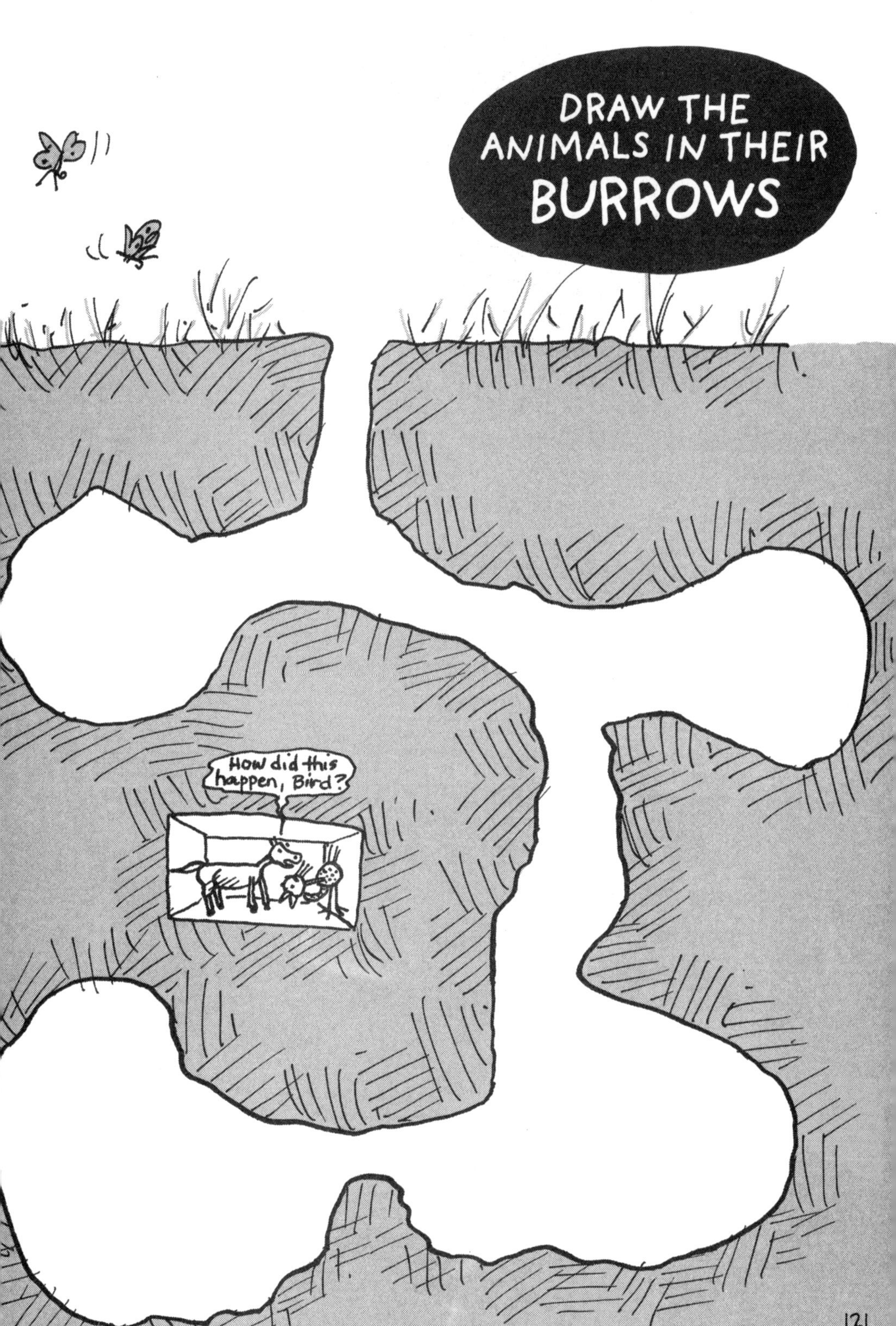
DRAW THE ANIMALS IN THEIR BURROWS
How did this happen, Bird?

DRAW
PEOPLE
IN THESE
HAMMOCKS
Z
Z

Z
Z

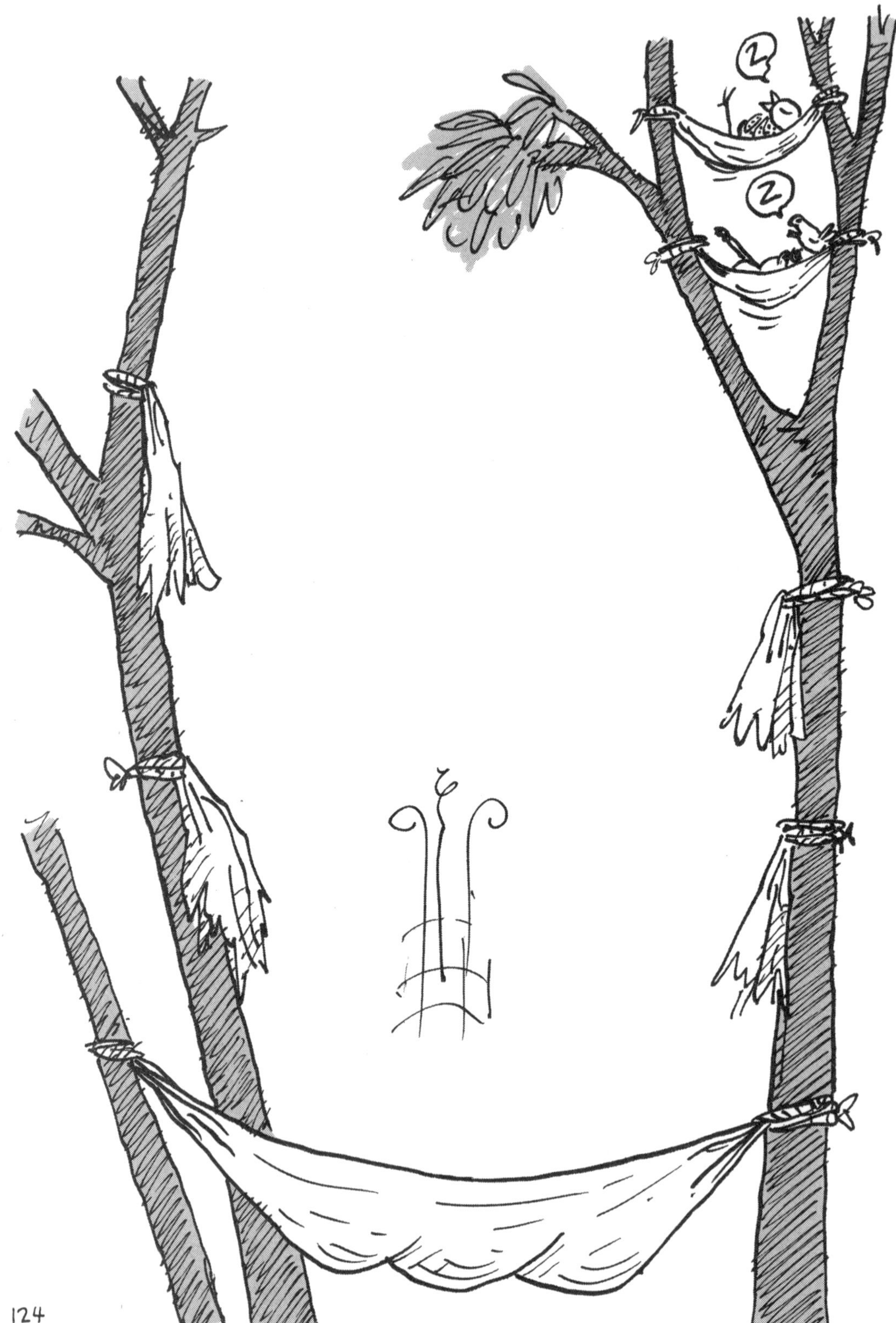

DRAW
THE CREATURES
WHO BELONG
TO THESE
EYES

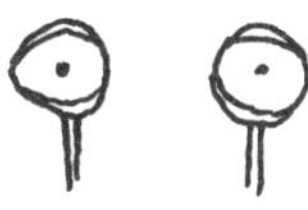

DRAW STARS! LOTS OF STARS!

Go crazy!

TORCH IN THE DARK

WHAT DO YOU SEE?

DRAW THE NIGHT-TIME EYES
Use white-out or a white texta or paint

TIME TO LEAVE!

Pack up all the stuff on top of the car

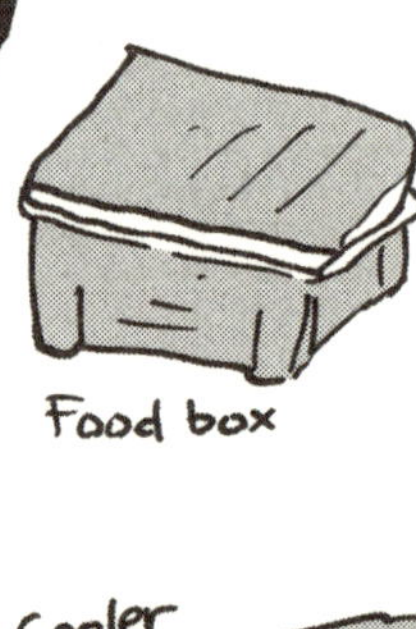

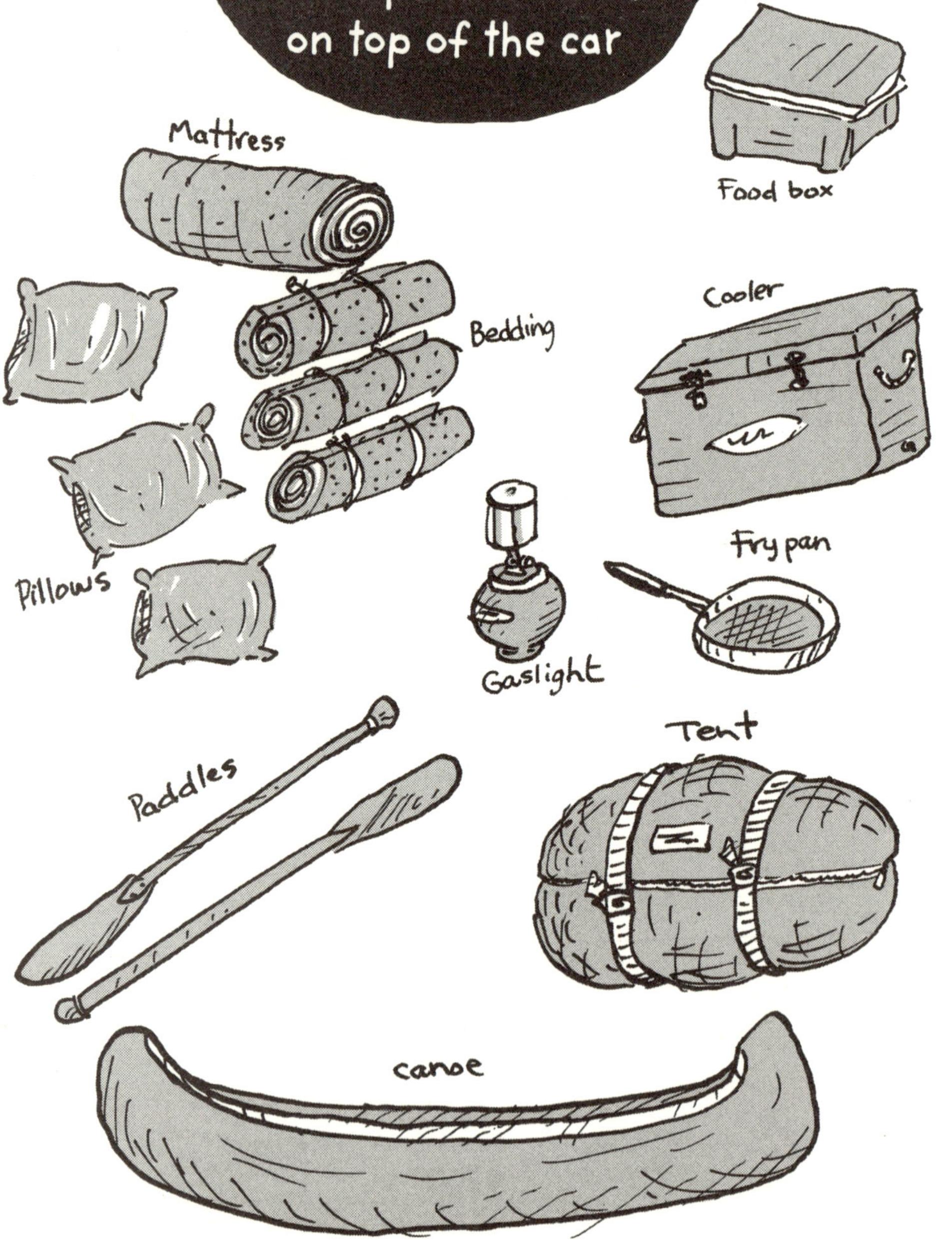
Mattress
Food box
Bedding
Cooler
Pillows
Fry pan
Gaslight
Tent
Paddles
canoe

SNOW TIME! FIND THE . . .

INGS TO ND:
Flying head • Spooky cloud • Skiing Santa • Duckling • Frog • Girl with missing tooth • Monkey • Snake • Dracula • Fish • Extra Terrestial • Warning sign • Snowboarding Wombat • Smart bird • Rhinoceros • Elvis • Queen of England •
I'm flying
BUMPER
BUMPER
HO! Ho! Ho!
ARGH!
EEEK!
Oh, the humanity

WHAT
TO WEAR
in the snow
BIRD
HORSE

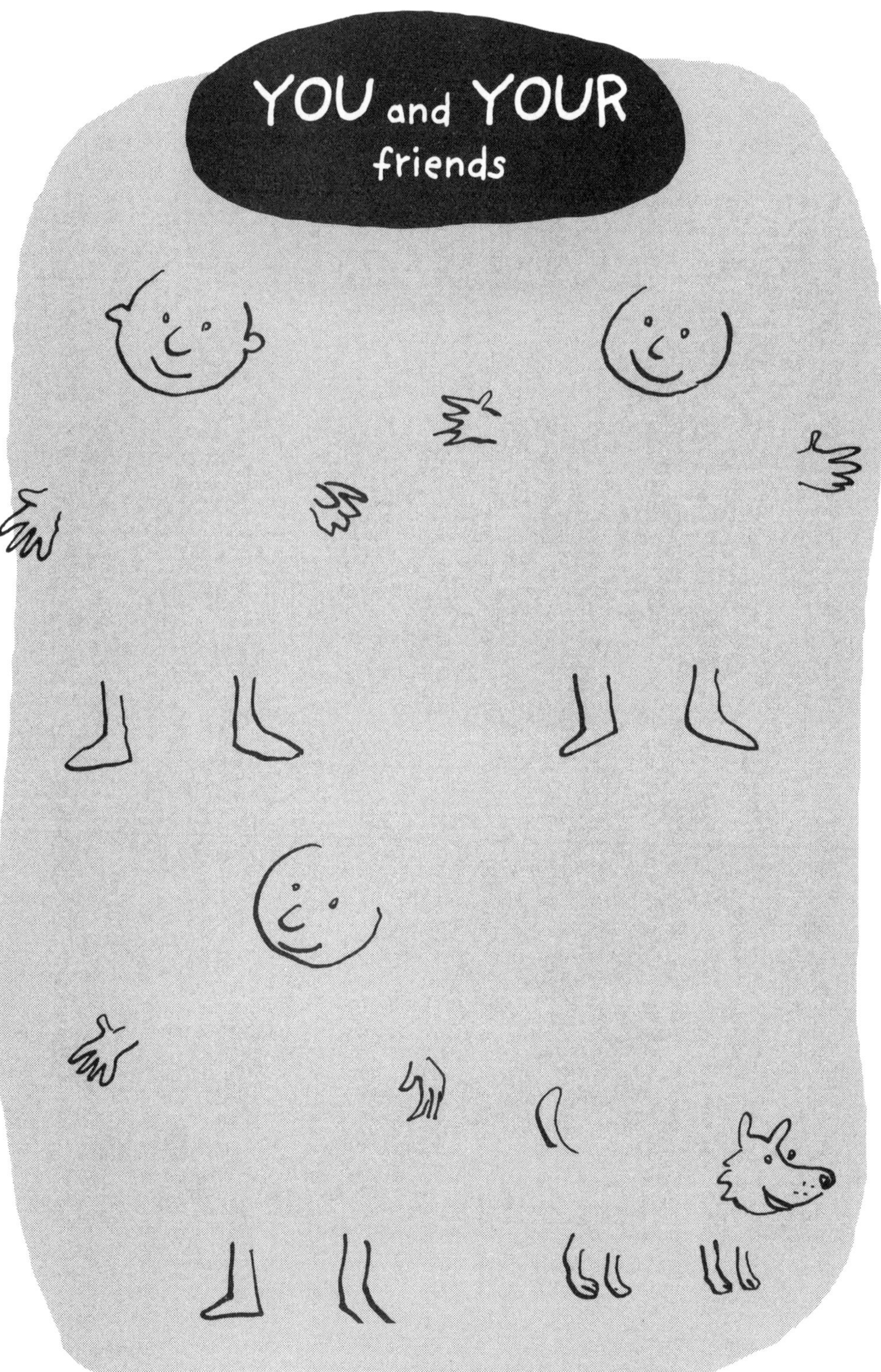
YOU and YOUR
friends

SNOWFLAKE SHAPES

Look at these and then draw some more

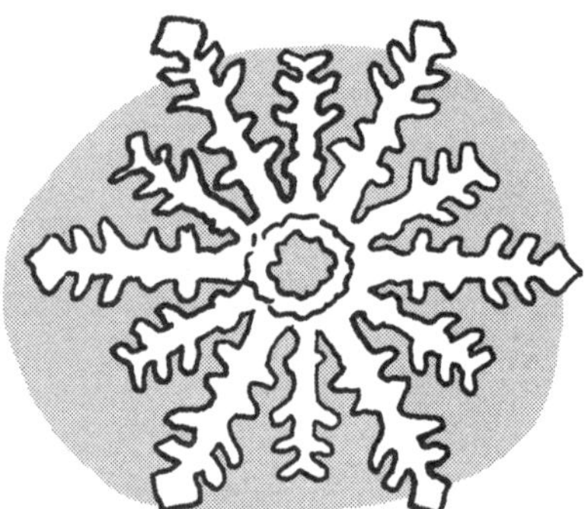

DRAW THEM BIG
RATHER THAN SMALL

EXPRESSIONS
ON FACES

NOW TRY SOME OF YOUR OWN.
WRITE WHAT THEY ARE

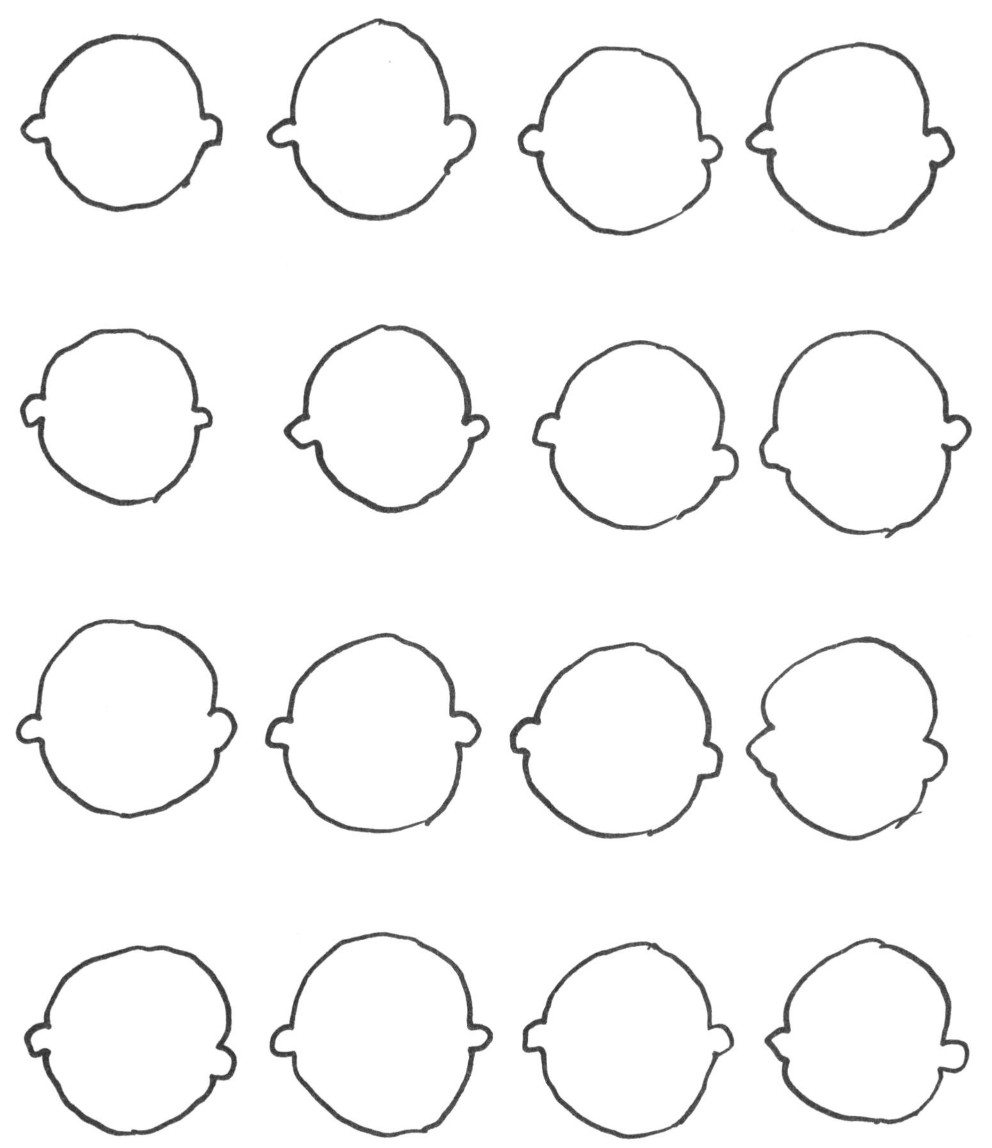

DRAW PEOPLE ON THE SKI LIFT

Some of them have dropped a glove
or a ski or a hat

Bird help!!
Hi, Horse.

DRAW PEOPLE SKIING DOWN THE MOUNTAIN

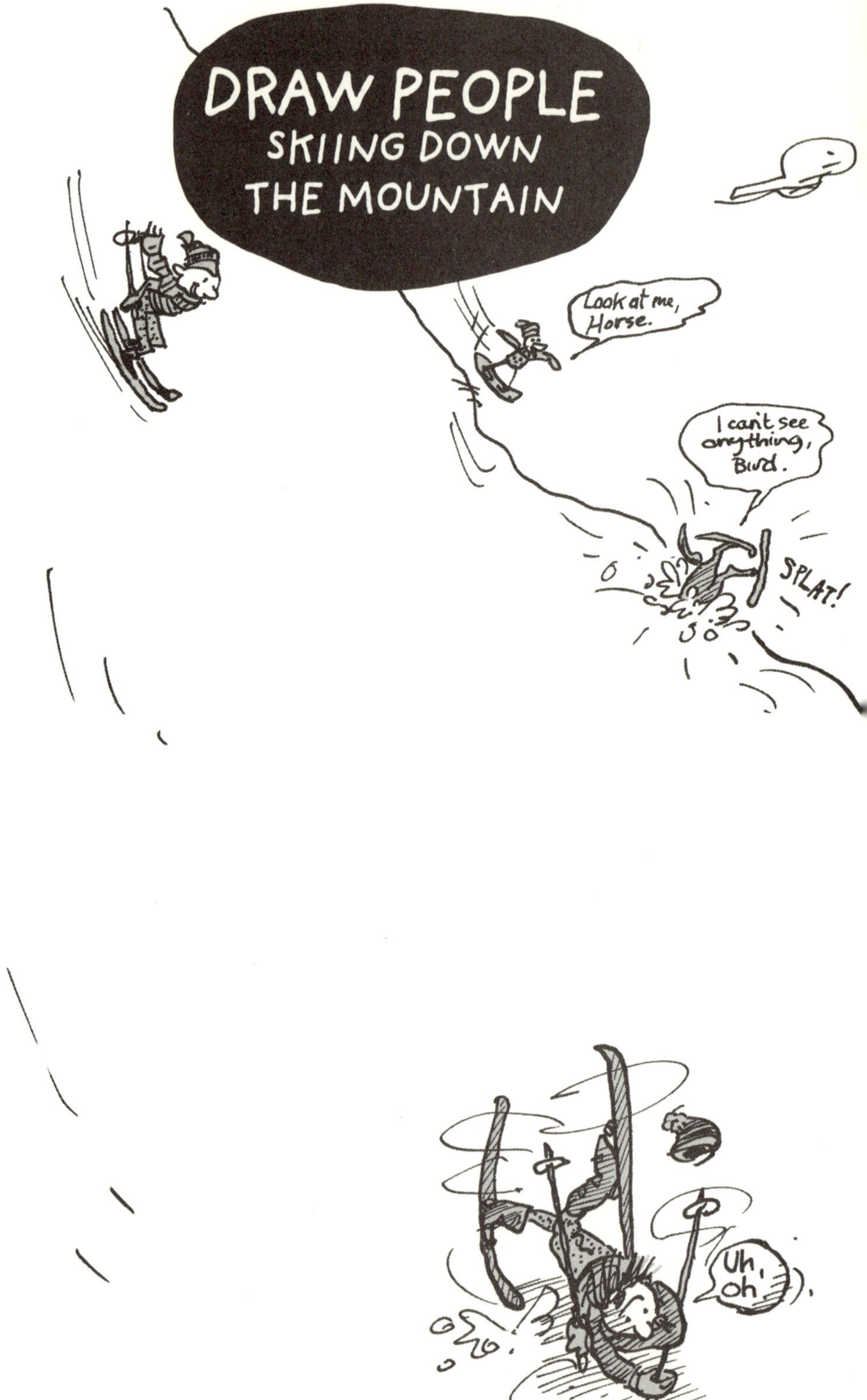

Look at me, Horse.

I can't see anything, Bird.

SPLAT!

THIS IS A POLE
DO NOT HIT YOUR HEAD ON THIS POLE

DRAW MORE SKIERS AND SNOWBOARDERS IN THIS PICTURE

NO!

SKI RACE
Which skier made it home?
1
2
3
4
5
6

Yeti
ARGH!

SNOW STORM. MIST. LOW CLOUD. IT'S A WHITE -OUT!

Can you find any people in this picture? (answer below)

May be they are all dressed in white.

I can't see anyone.

ANSWER: NO!

MAKE YOUR OWN SNOWMAN

BIRD and HORSE

YOU

Put clothes on your snowman

SNOW TRACKS

Match the tracks to the creatures

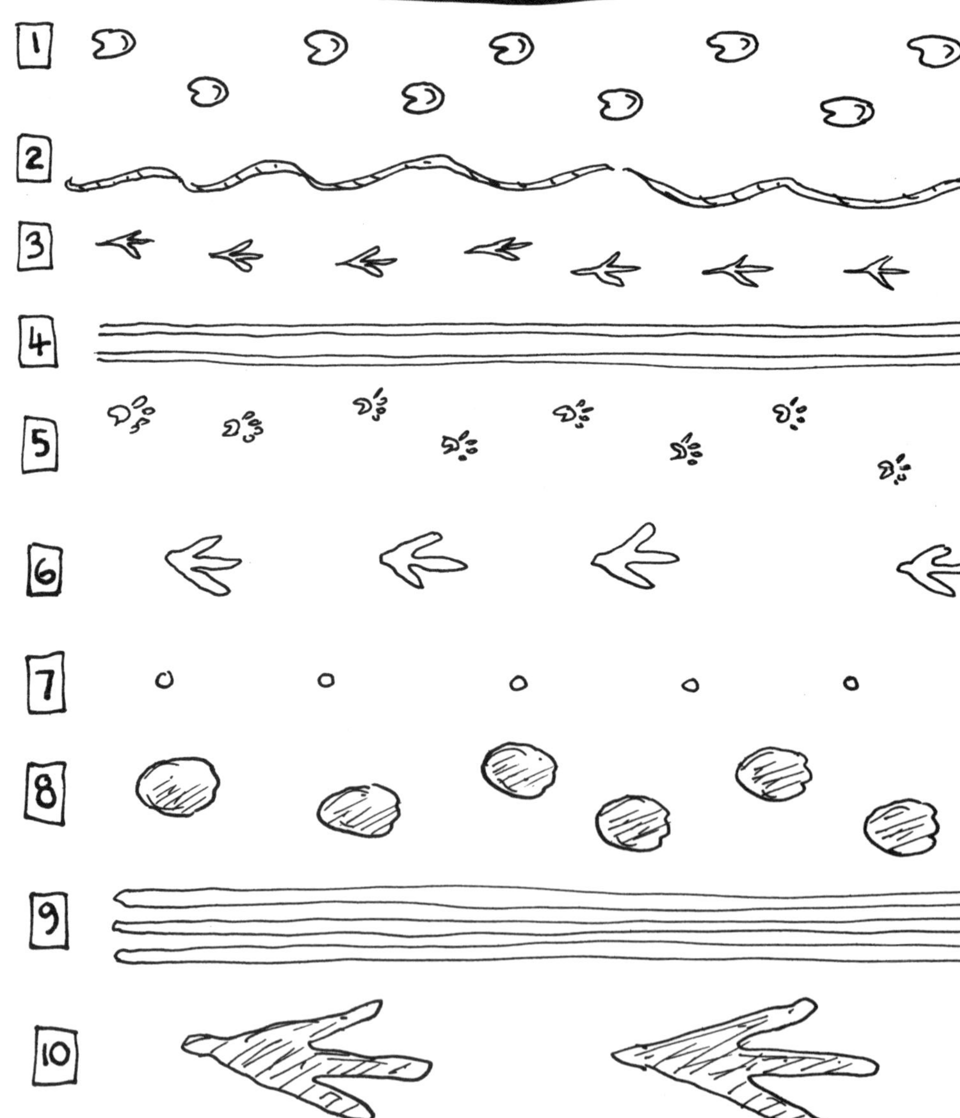

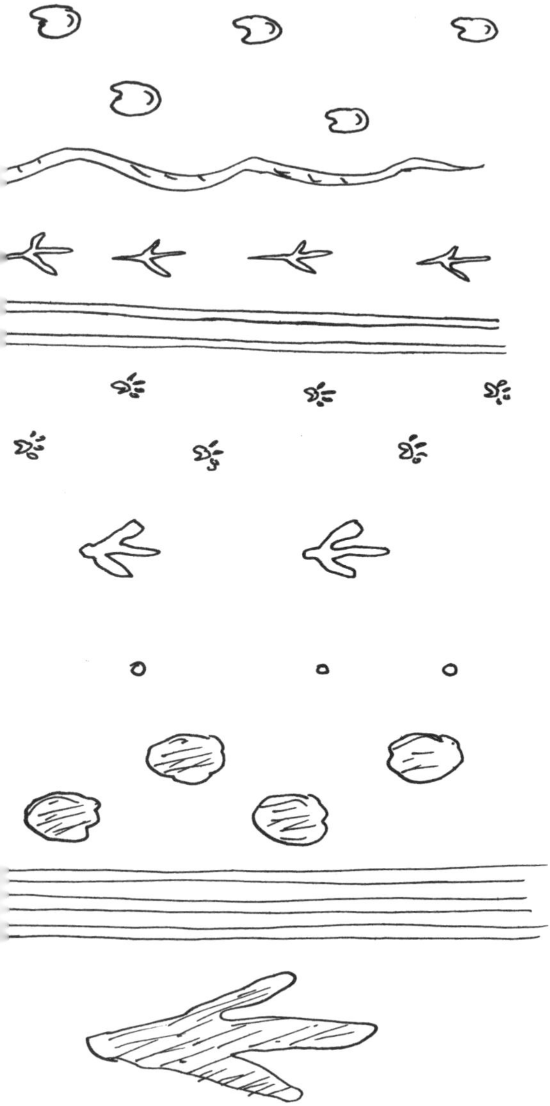

CREATURES

Put the matching number in the box

- DOG ☐
- HORSE ☐
- BIRD ☐
- EMU ☐
- POGO STICK ☐
- ELEPHANT ☐
- SNAKE ☐
- SKIER ☐
- THREE-LEGGED SKIER ☐
- T-REX ☐

CAN YOU DRAW AN ABOMINABLE SNOWMAN (YETI)?

YOU

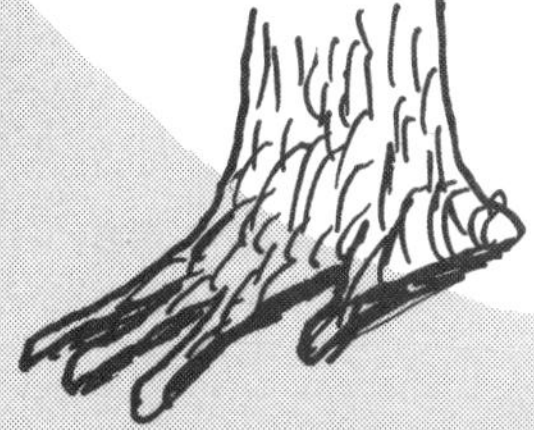

WHAT DO YOU LOVE OR HATE ABOUT THE SNOW? Tick the box

WRITE THINGS YOU LOVE OR HATE ABOUT THE SNOW AND SKIING

MATCH THE TOPS AND BOTTOMS OF THE CREATURES

That's the fifth time I've fallen over.

FARM STAY
FIND THE . . .

THINGS TO FIND:

- 2 emus •
- High goat •
- Farmhouse •
- Bulldozer •
- 5 llamas •

Farmer on a tractor • Cow tunnel through hill • Duck with 4 ducklings • Milking shed • Duck with hat • Flock of ibis • Hay bales • Apple tree • Scarecrow • 4 horses • Frog pond • Cook with bread • Barking farm dog • BBQ • Water tank • Active volcano • 3 sheep • Bull dozing • Wheat harvester • Snake • Water bird with fish •

THE BODY STARTS WITH 2 CIRCLES.

SO DOES THE HEAD. ONE BIG, ONE SMALL.

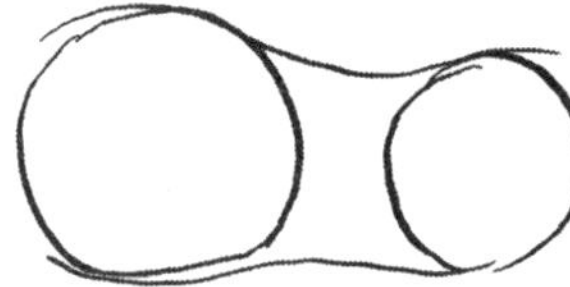

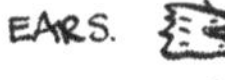

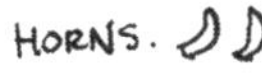

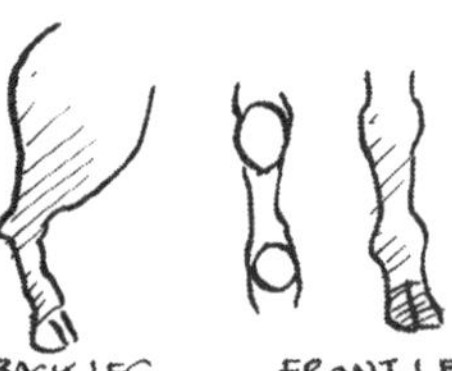

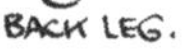

FRONT LEG.

UDDER.

WANT TO SEE MORE COWS RUNNING, JUMPING, SLEEPING?

GO TO GOOGLE IMAGES...

TYPE IN "COW"

AND YOU'LL GET 1000 COWS TO LOOK AT.

NOW TRY SOME
OF YOUR OWN

HOW TO DRAW A PIG

LIKE THE COW, THE PIG'S BODY STARTS WITH TWO CIRCLES.

PIG'S EAR.

PIG'S LEG.

PIG ON BIKE ... STICK FIGURE FIRST.

NOW TRY SOME
OF YOUR OWN

HOW TO DRAW A TRACTOR

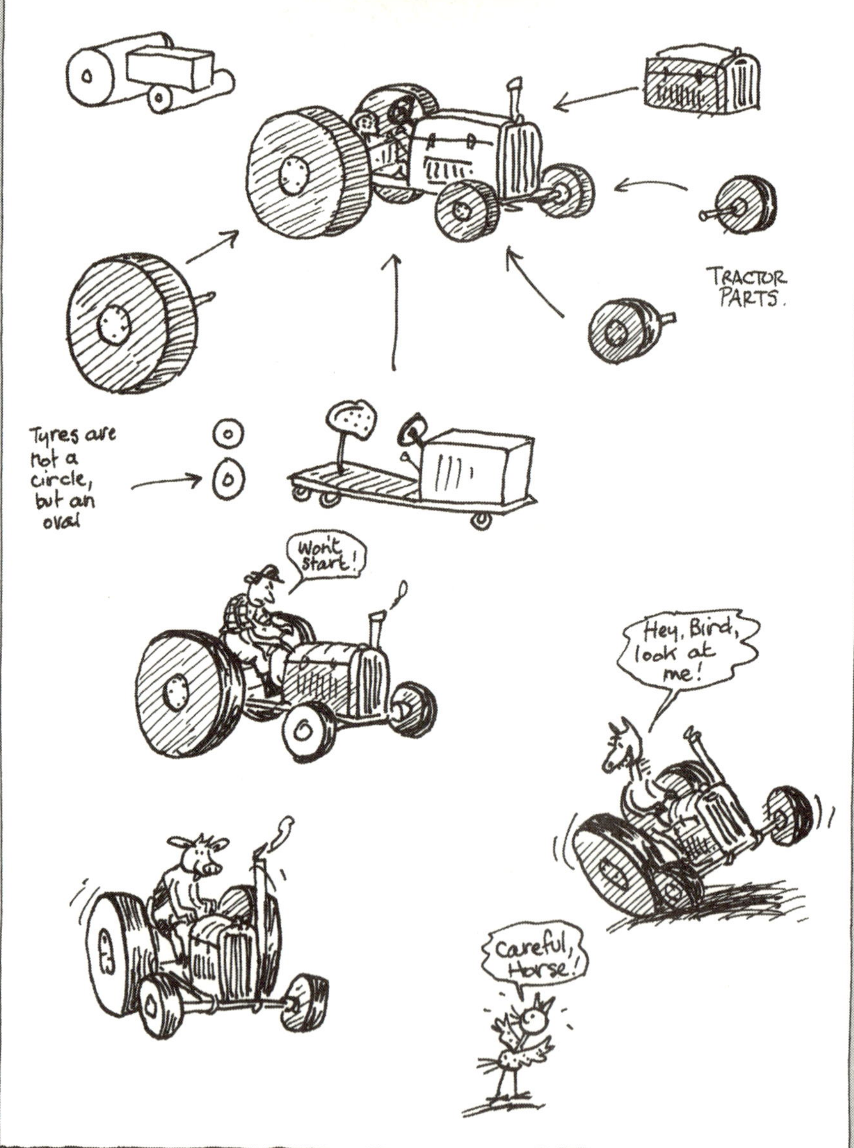

NOW **DRAW**
YOUR OWN TRACTOR
with a cow driving

DRAW A COW LIFTING
A TRACTOR DRIVEN BY A PIG
YAY!

PUT A COW IN A PLANE (FLYING!)

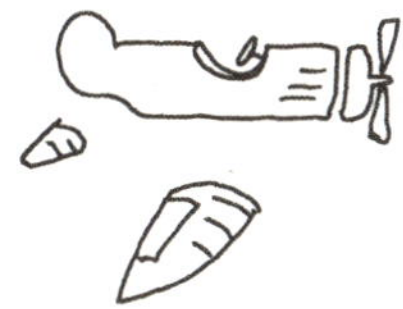
The bits of a plane.

OKAY!
DRAW A TRACTOR
CARRIED BY A COW
CARRIED BY A PIG

DRAW
COWS IN LOTS
OF DIFFERENT
FLYING
MACHINES

THEY'VE GONE CRAZY ON THE FARM! ALL THE ANIMALS ARE FLYING
This is fun, Bird.

Draw the acrobat sheep

MAKING NUMBERS

1
ONE

2
TWO

3
THREE

4
FOUR

5
FIVE

SIX

7
SEVEN

9
NINE

10
TEN

FARM ANIMALS
PIG
HORSE
GOAT
FROG
SHEEP
LLAMA
COW
BULL
DOG
FISH
YABBY
BLUE WREN

NOISES MADE BY FARM ANIMALS.
Draw the animal and the noise
PIG

nk!

BLORT!
YABBY

BIRDS,
BIRDS,
BIRDS
Count the number of eggs

See page 300 for the answer!

FROG CHORUS . . . but one frog is not singing.

Can you find it?

THE COW JUMPED OVER THE MOON
The horse jumped over the bird.

PUT YOURSELF ON THE RODEO HORSE

MATCH
EACH FARM ANIMAL WITH ITS PRODUCT

1	COW	A	STRAWBERRY	1
2	SHEEP	B	COB OF CORN	2
3	CHICKEN	C	HOUSE OF STRAW	3
4	WHEAT	D	MEAT	4
5	GRAPES	E	EGG	5
6	PIG	F	BREAD	6
7	DOG	G	WOOLLEN CLOTHES	7
8	PLANT	H	POO	8
9	CORN	I	MILK	9
10	TURKEY	J	WINE	10

THE DONKEY IS BEING STUBBORN. HOW MANY PEOPLE DOES IT TAKE TO PULL HIM HOME?
Horse
Birds
ADD MORE PEOPLE
Hey, everyone! The farmer and the donkey are having a fight!!

DRAW THE
ROOSTER
CROWING
AT DAWN

SUN

DRAW WHAT
THE BULL
IS CHASING

MOTHER DUCK HAS LOST HER DUCKLINGS.
CAN YOU FIND ALL 26 DUCKLINGS?

WAK!
WAK!
WAK!
NO DUCKLINGS HERE

HOME AND NEIGHBOURHOOD

How many cats and dogs can you find?

The answer is on page 300.

I am hot.
How to stay
HOT
on cool days

I'm cool!
ICE
How to stay COOL on hot days

DRAW A MAP of your neighbourhood and your house

THINGS ON THE MAP:

Draw some of your own symbols ↓

PLACES
TO READ
A BOOK

BUILD
A TREE
HOUSE

LOOKING AT CATERPILLARS

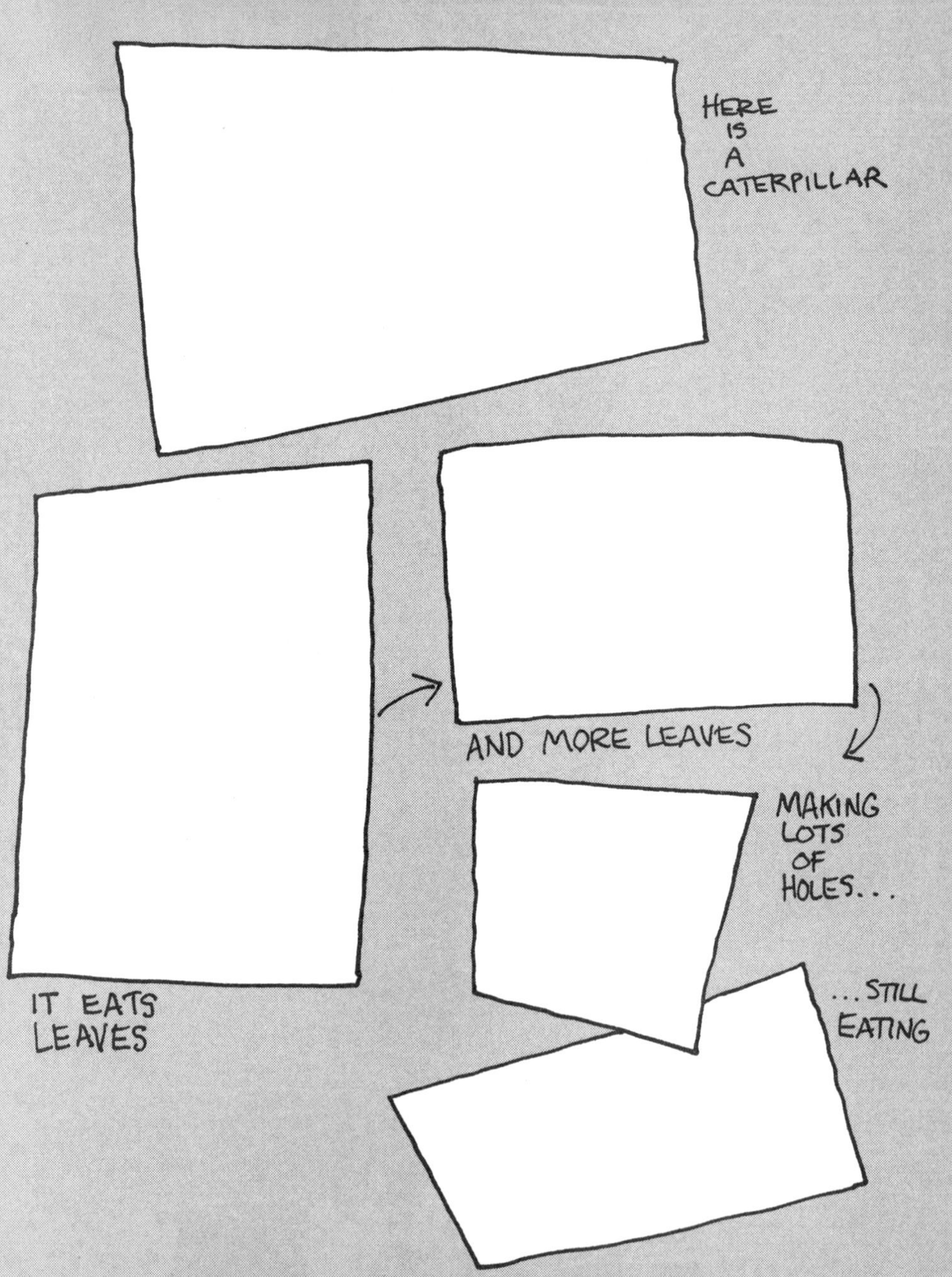

IT MAKES A COCOON
THEN FALLS ASLEEP
AFTER A LONG TIME IT WAKES AND BREAKS OUT...
...IT'S NOW A BUTTERFLY
IT FLIES AWAY

WHAT IS ITS ADDRESS?

WWW.

DRAW THE COMPUTER GAME

BORED AT HOME?
INVENT BACKYARD SPORTS

YARD TO YARD TRAMPOLINING

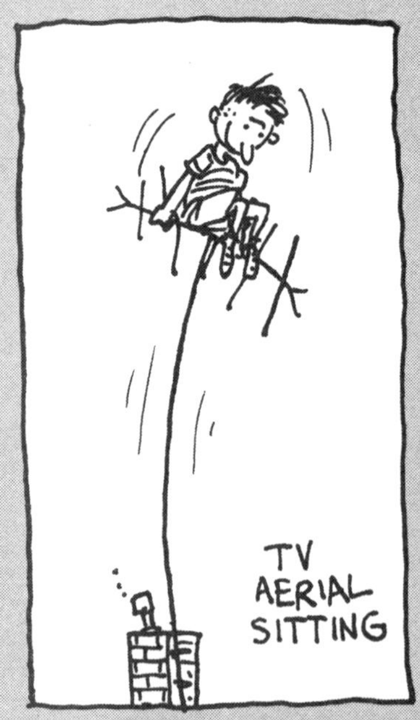

TV AERIAL SITTING

DESIGN YOUR

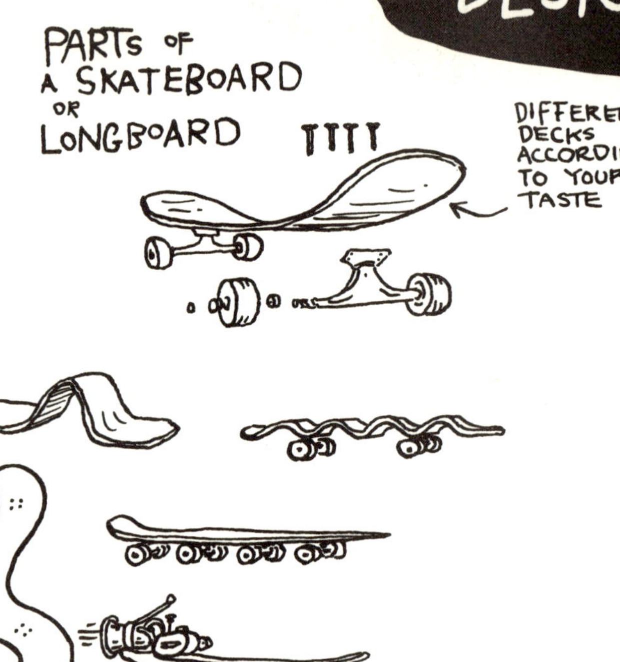

PARTS OF
A SKATEBOARD
OR
LONGBOARD
DIFFERENT
DECKS
ACCORDING
TO YOUR
TASTE
Jet pack

OWN SKATEBOARD

WAYS TO FALL OFF

YOUR SKATEBOARD. DRAW SOME OF YOUR OWN

DOG	CAT	BIRD
FRIDGE	WASHING MACHINE	DRYER
CHAIR	PHONE	BROOM

VACUUM	BRUSH + PAN	TV
TV REMOTE	KEY	CUP
TAPE DISPENSER	SCISSORS	VASE

THINGS I LIKE / HATE
(Tick the Box)

BEING CLOSE TO YOUR FRIENDS

☐ LOVE HATE ☐

MAKING CUBBIES OUTSIDE

☐ LOVE HATE ☐

NOT HAVING TO PACK TO GO AWAY

☐ LOVE HATE ☐

HOLIDAY CAMP

☐ LOVE HATE ☐

SWIMMING LESSONS

☐ LOVE HATE ☐

DAILY TV PROGRAMS

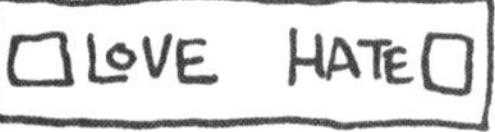

☐ LOVE HATE ☐

FEEDING THE NEIGHBOUR'S PETS

☐ LOVE HATE ☐

THE NEIGHBOUR'S POOL

☐ LOVE HATE ☐

WATCHING NEXT DOOR'S MASSIVE TV

☐ LOVE HATE ☐

WATCHING ENDLESS SPORT ON TV
LOVE HATE
BACKYARD SPORT
LOVE HATE
BOING!
SETTING A NEW TRAMPOLINE BOUNCES RECORD
LOVE HATE
HOT CHOCCY IN PJs ON COUCH
LOVE HATE
BEING IN YOUR PJs ALL DAY
LOVE HATE
COUCH AND DOONA CUBBIES
LOVE HATE
WATCHING PLAYSCHOOL AND SESAME STREET
COOKIES!
LOVE HATE
POPCORN AND PANCAKES ON THE COUCH
LOVE HATE
ARRGH!
NO!
MUM!
PLAYING MURDER IN THE DARK
EEK!
DAD!
HELP!
NOOOOOO!!
GOT YOU!
LOVE HATE

SWIMMING POOL
Which kid has lost his bathers?

DRAW 15 KIDS IN THE CUBBY

One bird.

And one horse.

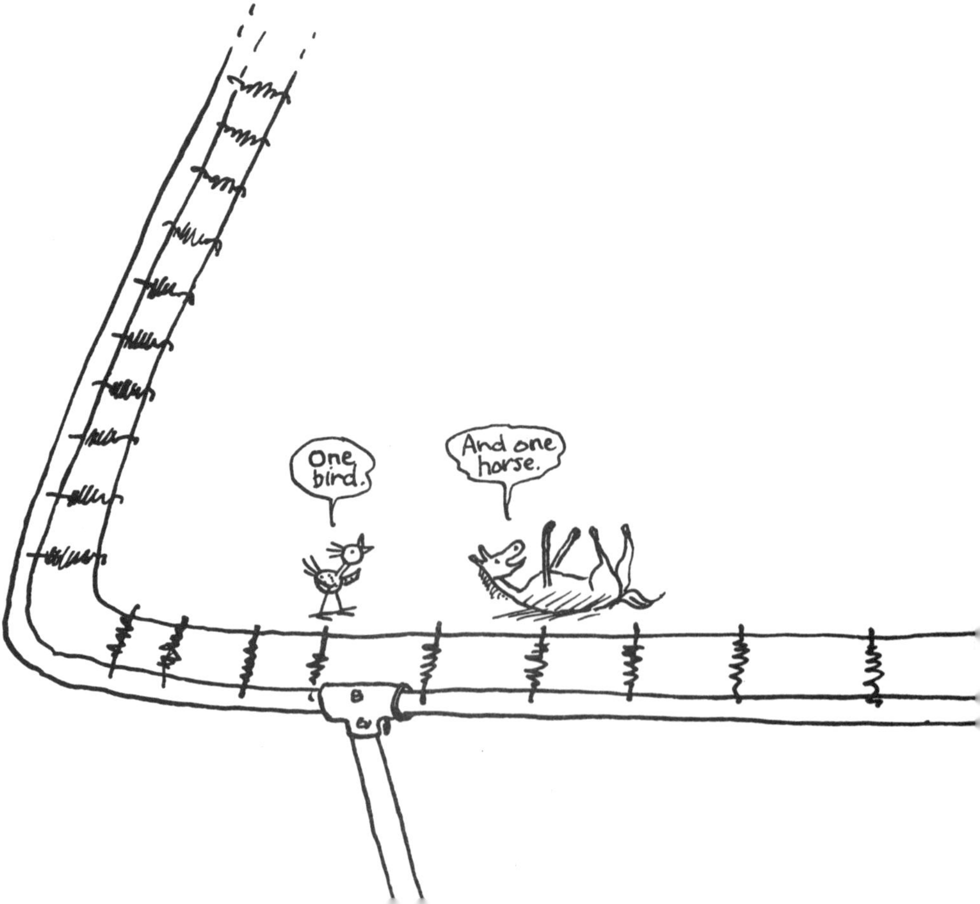

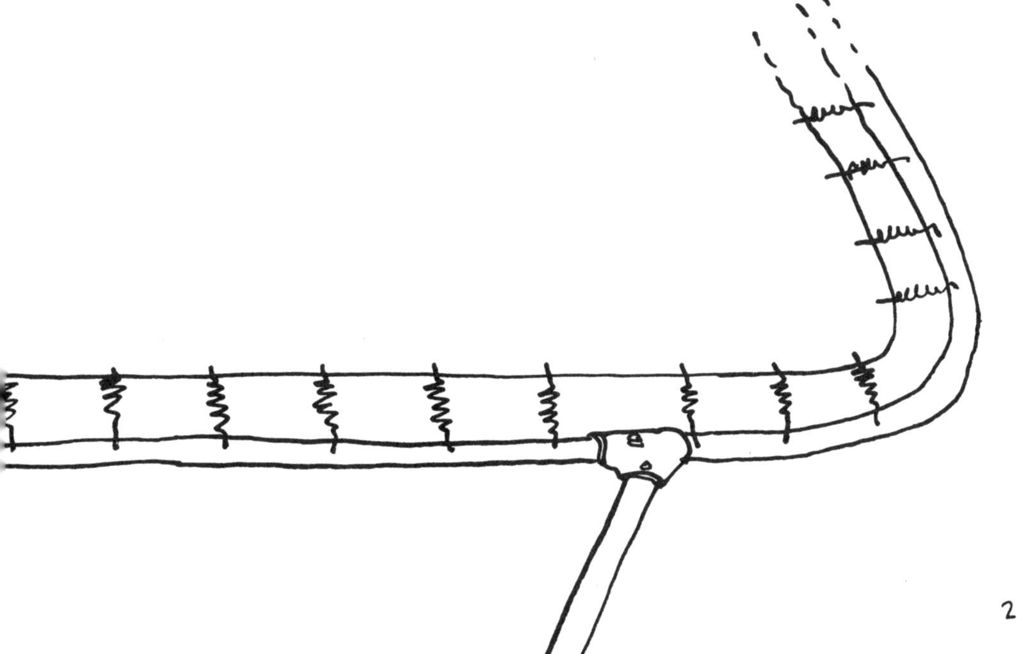

MOUNTAIN HORSERIDING

Find the . . .

THINGS TO FIND:

3 rabbits • Fish-shaped cloud • A cow pyramid • Falling horse • Collapsed cow pyramid • Rolling tractor • Tree house • Ski village • Sleeping horse and rider • Stubborn horse • Frog • Snake • 7 dwarves • Ogre with fish • Pig in wooden house • Wolf • Runaway horse • Angry ogre's wife • Kangaroo family • Giraffe •

HOW TO DRAW A CARTOON HORSE

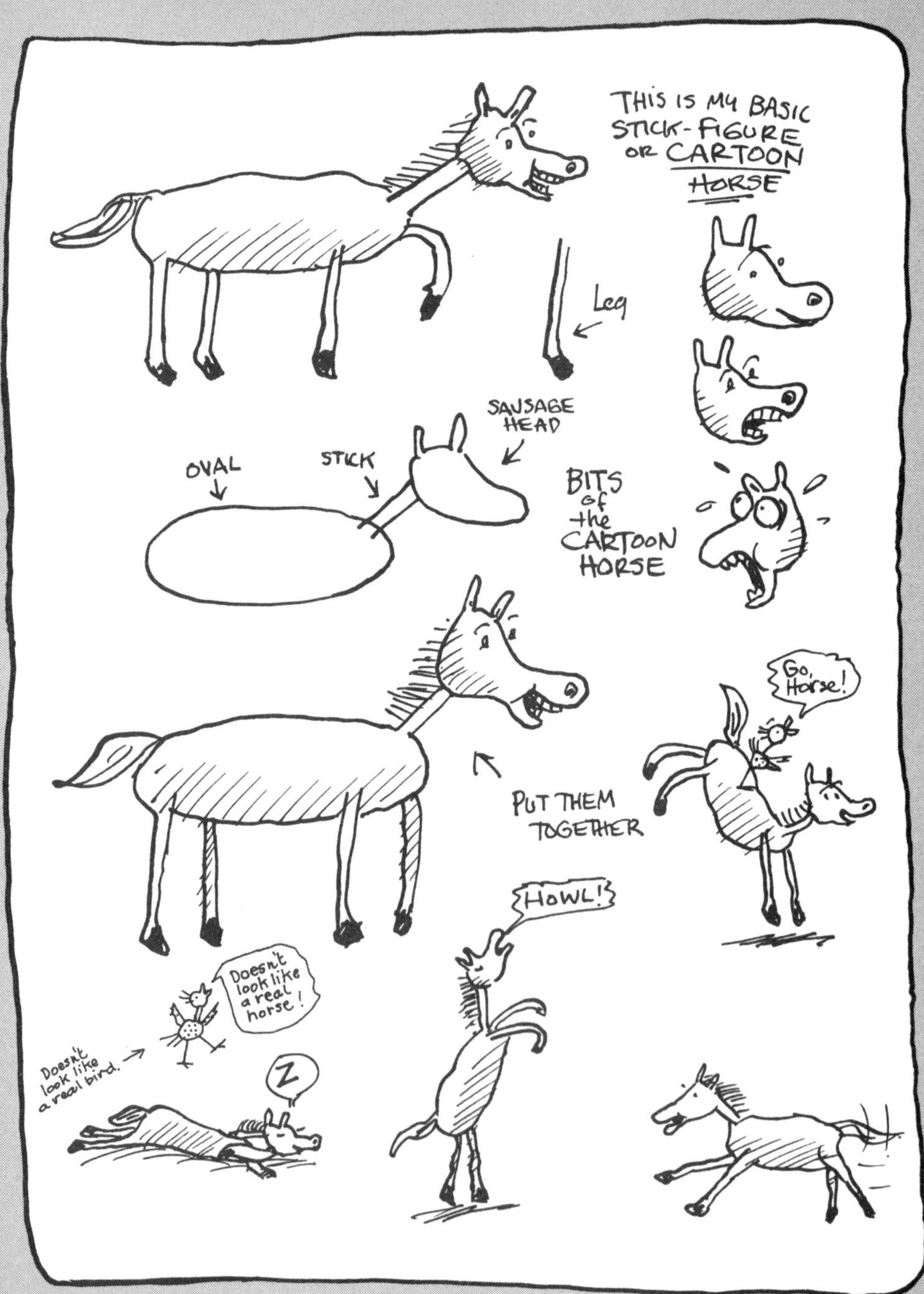

NOW YOU TRY

HOW A HORSE RUNS

YOU
DRAW!

DRAW
HORSES
WITH
SADDLES

NOW DRAW
HORSES WITH
RIDERS IN THE
SADDLES

WHAT ABOUT SOME VERY FANCY SADDLES?
Two-storey . . . Three-storey . . . with umbrellas . . . and drink dispenser . . . and cable TV

AND DRAW PEOPLE IN THOSE VERY FANCY SADDLES

And grumpy horses who hate fancy saddles and just want to run free in the mountains

Hello...

INVENT
WAYS TO GET
PHONE
RECEPTION IN THE
MOUNTAINS

DRAW THESE THINGS

SADDLE

DUCK

SUNSHINE

PINE TREE

GUM TREE

MUSHROOM

RAIN

EAGLE

CLOUD

A VERY LONG SNAKE

FISHERMAN

CHICKEN

FOX

TRACTOR

COW

MOWER

RIVER

WATERFALL

KANGAROO

10 THINGS TO DO WITH HORSES

YOU DRAW ANOTHER 7
(GO CRAZY!)

THE OLD HORSE
SWALLOWED AN OLD LADY
WHO SWALLOWED A CAT
WHO SWALLOWED A BIRD
WHO SWALLOWED
A FLY

YOU AND YOUR HORSE FALL OFF A CLIFF. LUCKILY YOU HAVE PARACHUTES!

DRAW SOME MORE THINGS

Very long hot dog

Saucepan

Fry pan

Kettle

Slushie

Milkshake

Chips

Fried egg

Prawn

Squid

BUMPER
B·B·Q
INC.

DRAW ALL THE FOOD ON THE BBQ
steak burgers
Potato wedges
Prawns
Mushrooms
Kebabs
Tomatoes
Grasshoppers
Blowfly
Fish fillets
sausages
chops
Vegie burgers

It's
POPCORN
night. Draw the popcorn popping. Lots + lots + lots + lots + lots + lots of popcorn popping!

YAY!
POPCORN
SAUCEPAN

WHAT IS INSIDE
A MOUNTAIN?

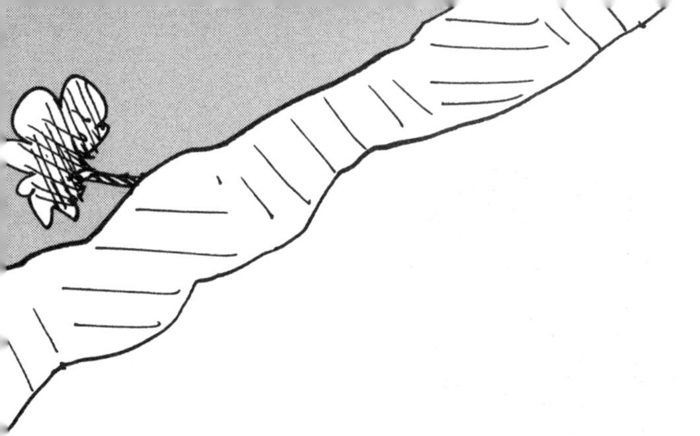

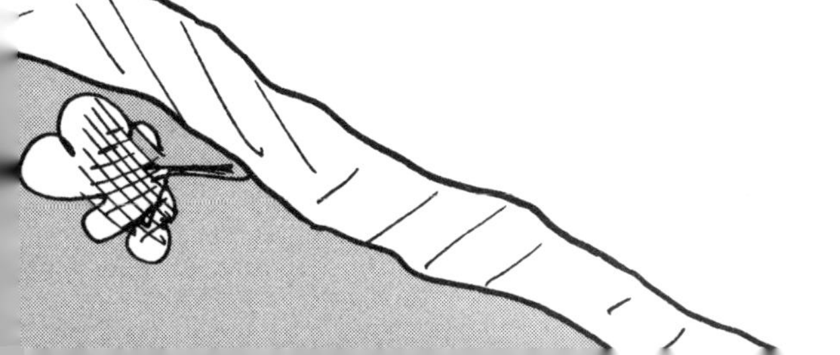

DID YOU KNOW?

Horses turn into horseflies. DRAW IT!

The horse eats a lot.

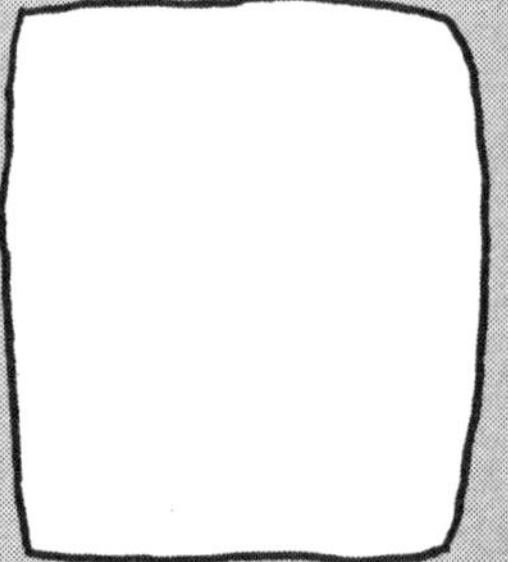

It gets tired.

It spins a cocoon and falls asleep inside.

The horse sleeps for 100 days.

Then it bursts out of the cocoon as a horsefly.

And the horsefly flies away.

THINGS A HORSE IS SCARED OF!
SNAKES IN THE GRASS
CROCODILE TREES

SPACE HOLIDAY
Find the ...
THINGS TO FIND:
Big banana •
Man with sore head •
Killer toaster •
Square planet •
Large hamburger •
Get me out of here.
OUCH.
00100.
0000.
NO!
Gasp!
514

A fork • Cup of coffee • Electric plug • Fountain pen • Astronaut asleep • Bike rider • Pirates • Aliens in a teacup • Dice • Big tongue • Superman • Soup man • Space horse • Cannonball • Falling astronaut • Bomb • Astronaut in inflatable boat • Pedal-powered spacecraft • Big fish • Singing astronaut • Monster • Kid surfing • Fried egg

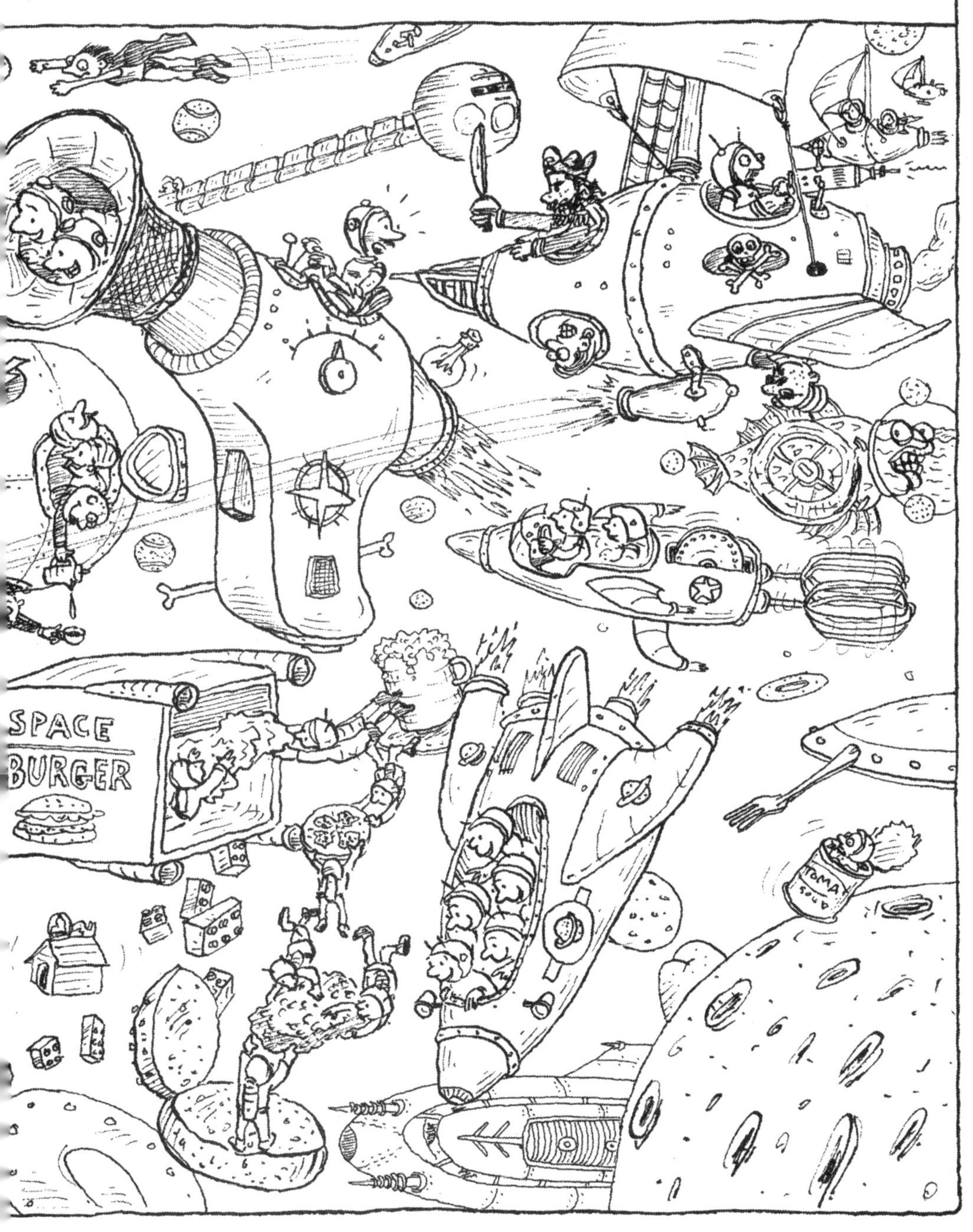

HOW TO GET INTO SPACE

Draw your ideas

MAKE
YOUR OWN
SPACESHIP

PIZZA in the
SPACESHIP
Draw all the
floating fillings

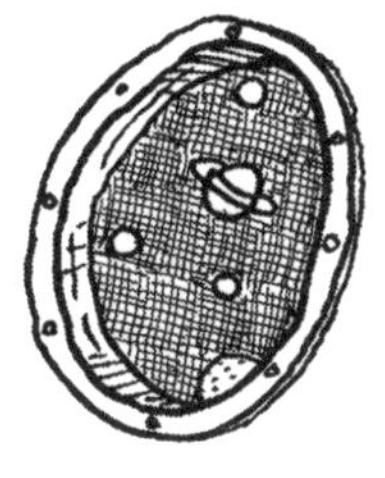

Imagine
zero gravity
IN YOUR HOUSE
Draw all your stuff
floating in the
house

NOW YOUR HOUSE

IS FLOATING AWAY

And your neighbours

SUN
M
V
E
M
PLANETS
Name them
J
S
U
N

LOOK OUT THE SPACESHIP WINDOW
What do you see?
Horse
Teabag
Thing
Bird
Doughnut
Spanner
potato chips

DRAW THE ALIENS HIDDEN BEHIND EACH OF THESE SPACE ROCKS

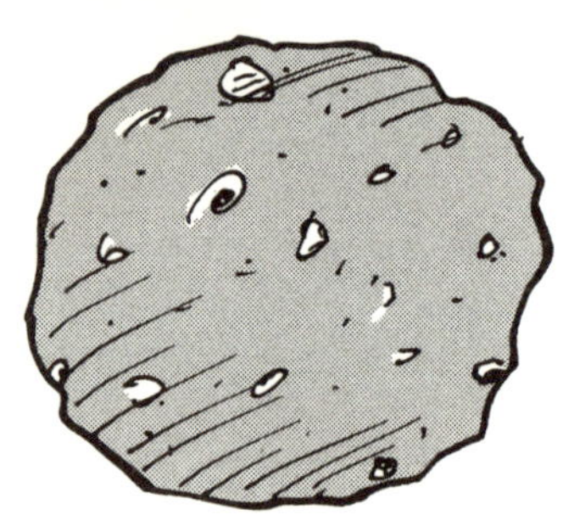

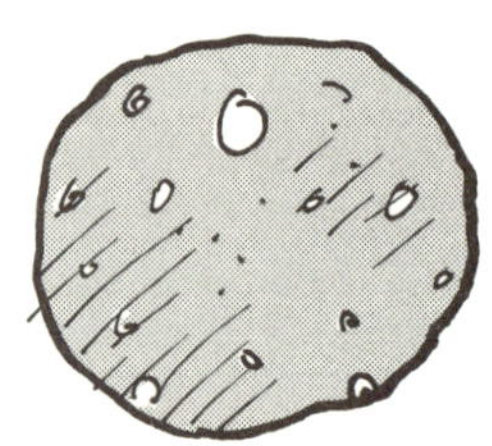

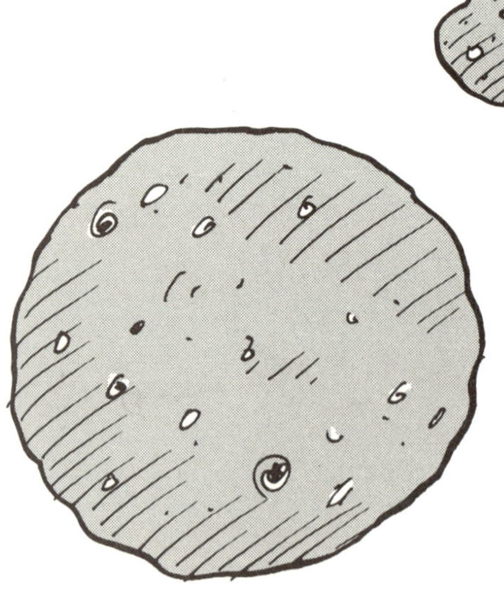

THIS SPACE MONSTER BABY
HAS LOST ITS DAD
Can you draw him?

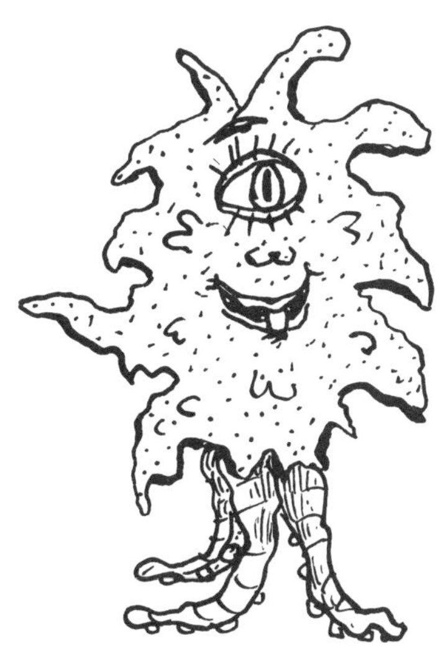

COLOURS
There are none in this book

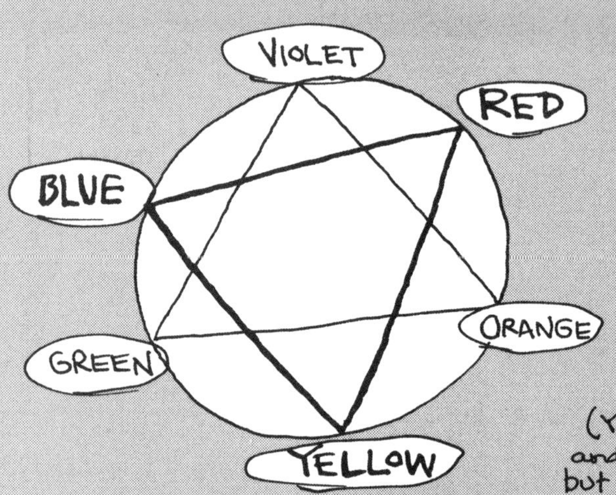

RED, BLUE + YELLOW ARE THE 3 PRIMARY COLOURS

GREEN, ORANGE + VIOLET ARE THE 3 SECONDARY COLOURS.

(You can make GREEN, ORANGE and VIOLET from other colours, but not RED, BLUE + YELLOW. They can't be made from others.)

GREEN IS MADE FROM BLUE + YELLOW
ORANGE IS MADE FROM YELLOW + RED
VIOLET IS MADE FROM RED + BLUE

THAT'S ALL YOU NEED TO KNOW ABOUT COLOURS.
(I might have lied!!!)

SPACESHIP
Colour by numbers

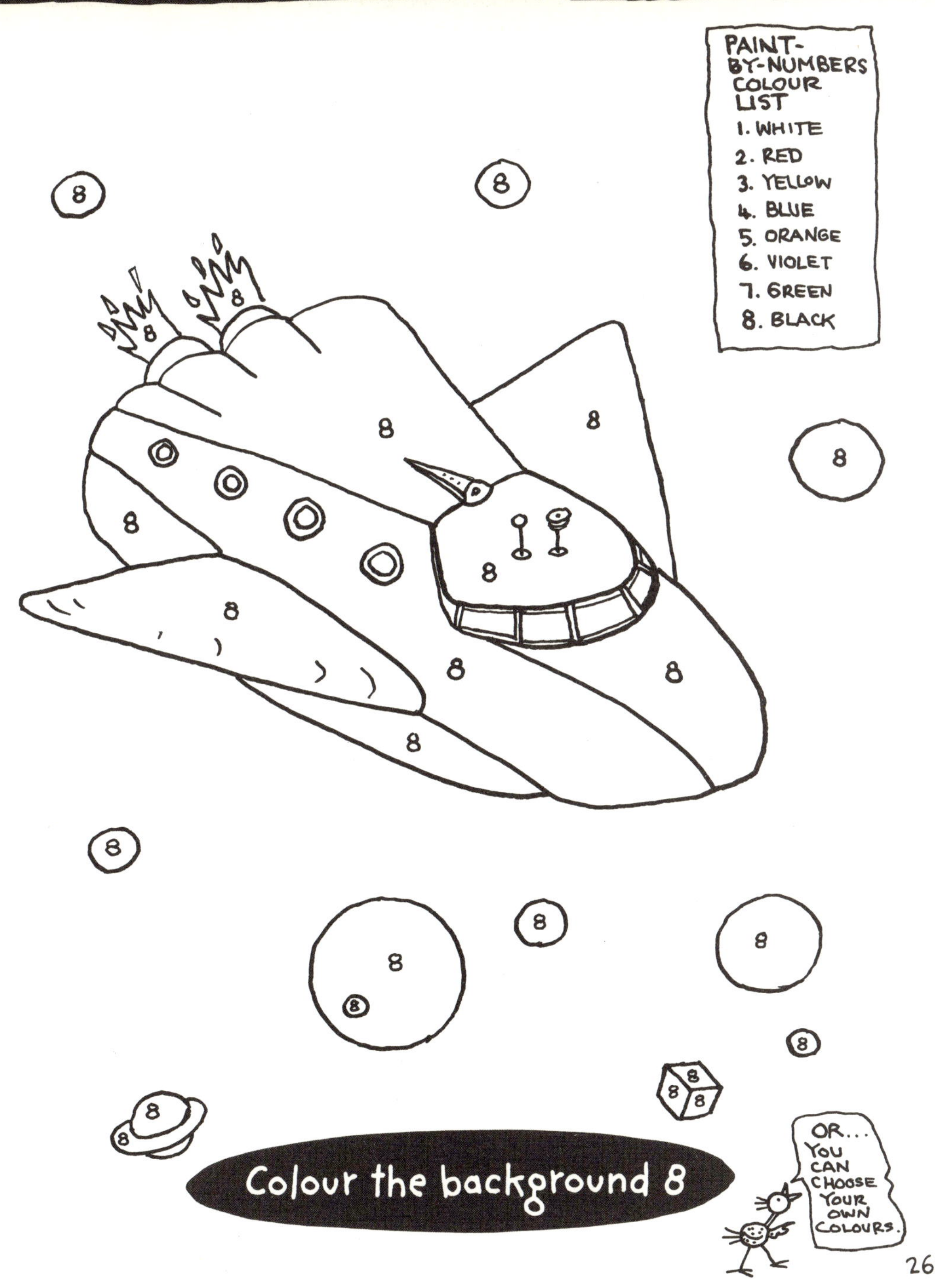

TAKING YOUR PET SPIDER INTO SPACE
(Clothes, food, containment)

SHOW THE SPIDER TAKING A SPACE WALK

SPACE WALK CONFUSION

Which spaceship does each astronaut belong to?

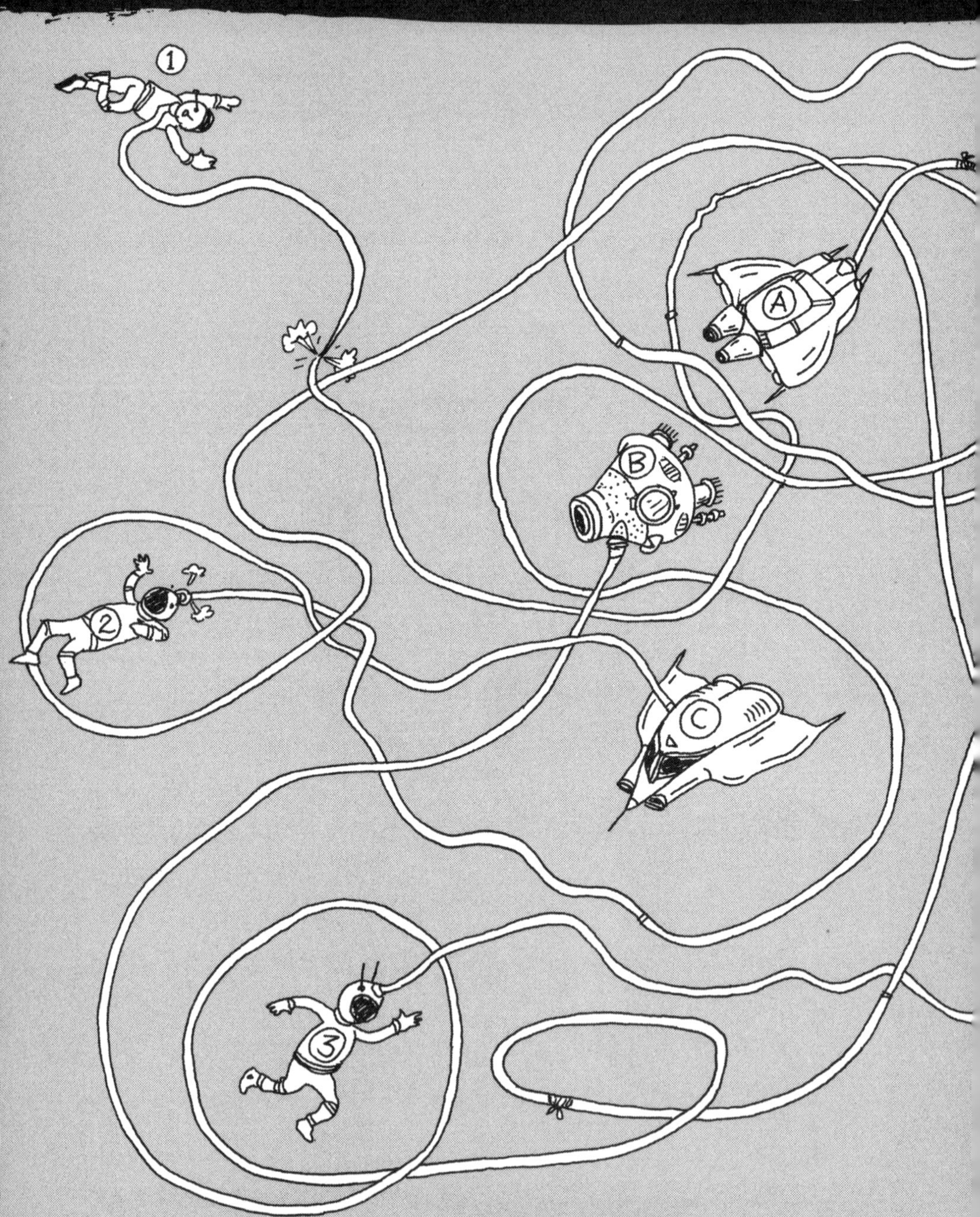

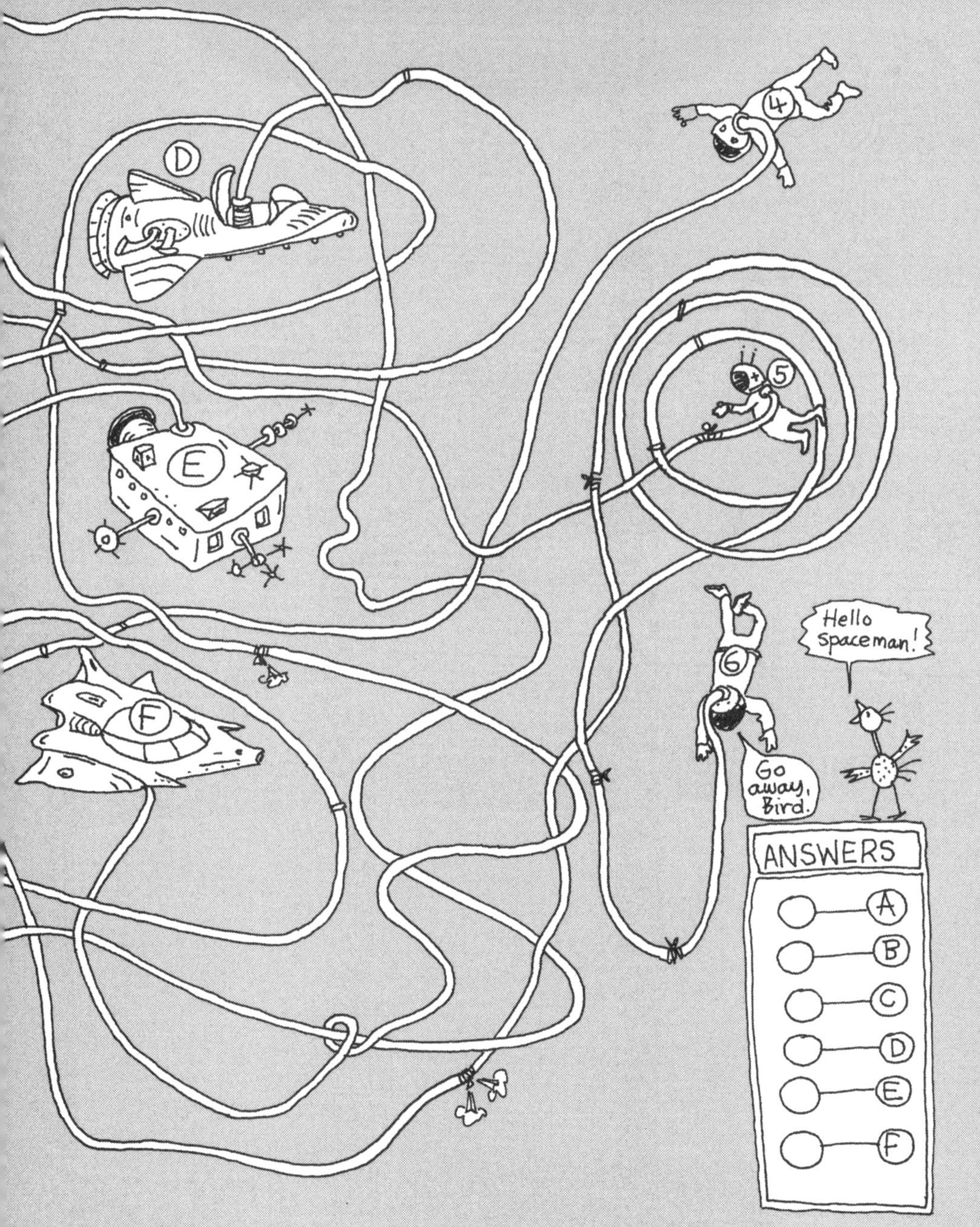
D
E
F
4
5
6
Hello spaceman!
Go away, Bird.
ANSWERS
A
B
C
D
E
F

SPACE JAM

Fill in the spaces between space craft

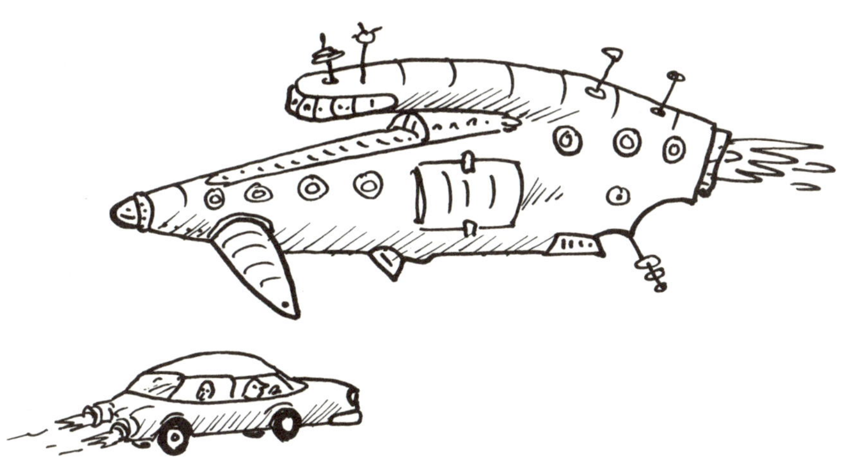

I can't breathe.

BIG
BAD ALIENS ARE
IN THE CAGES
What do they
look like?

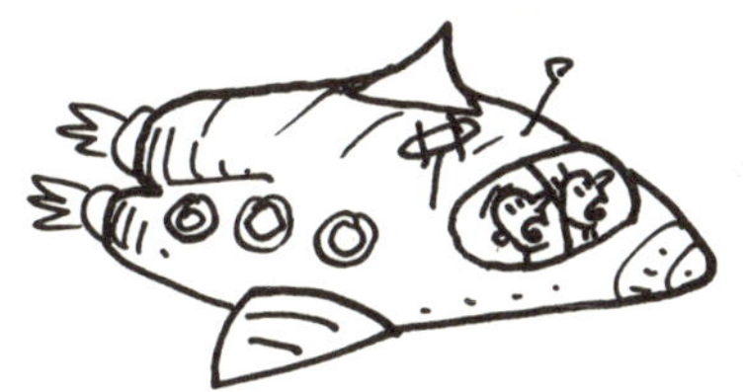

It's like a squid but an alien.
BEWARE
OF THE FLOATING
SQUID ALIEN

YOU HAVE CRASH-LANDED ON A STRANGE PLANET

WHAT DOES IT LOOK LIKE?

You are flying
BACK TO
EARTH
What does it
look like?
Blah.
Blah,
blah..

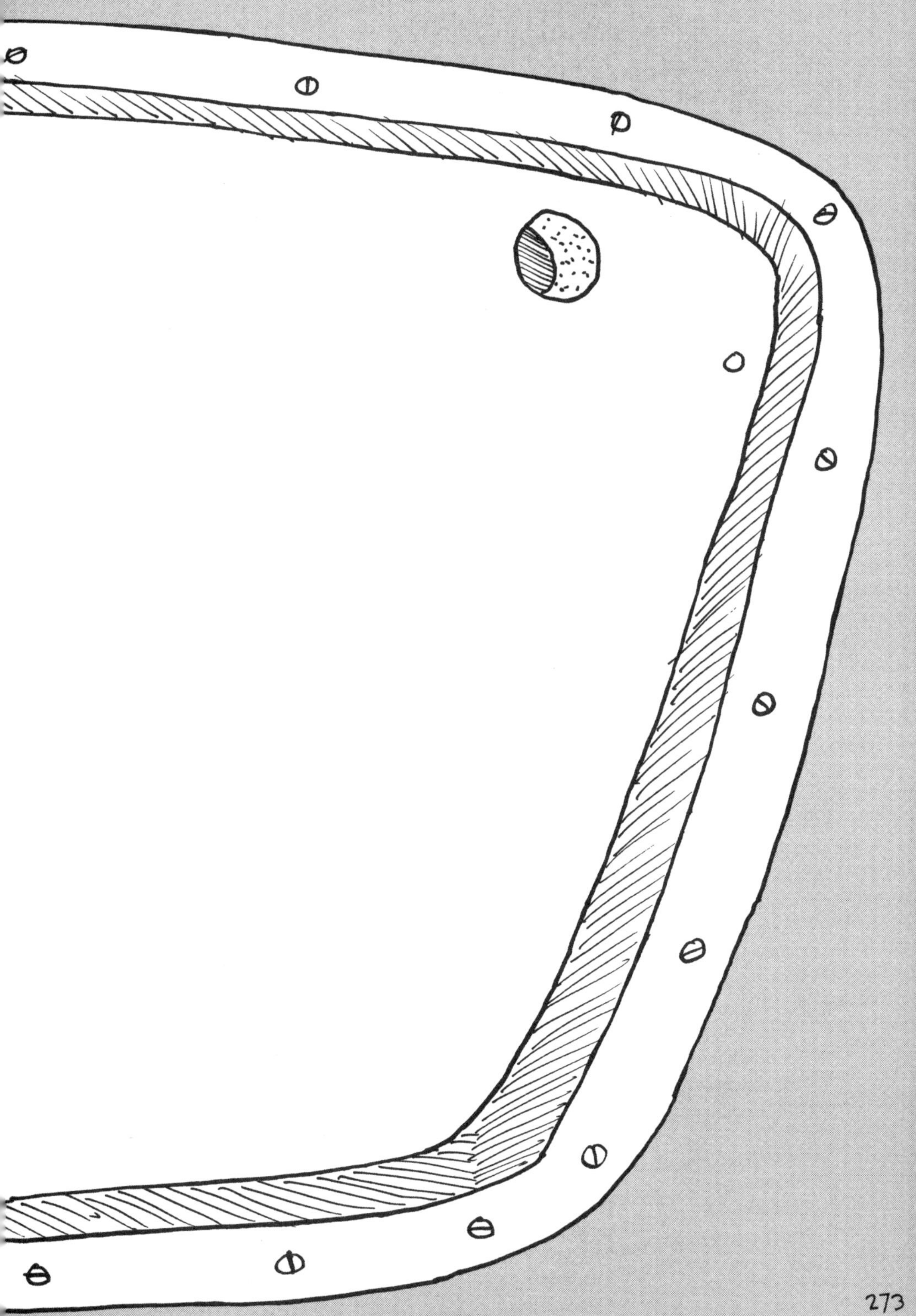

On returning to earth you fly around the moon 3 times, circle the earth twice, go through the middle of the planet doughnut, back around the moon, twice around the bird, in the horse's

mouth and out the other end, around Saturn, through Jupiter, twice around Mars, up to Venus, around my letterbox, past Mrs Kawolski, and land on your town. IT'S EASY!

END OF the HOLIDAYS
Find all the things in this picture
THINGS TO FIND:
Snake wrestling •
Chicken teacher •
Gorilla teacher •
Tall girl •
Romeo •
BOOM!
BUK!
Let me out.
Hey, Bully, Look at me.
Urk!
a

School elephant asleep • Giant hotdog • Soccer ball in mouth • Quicksand • Girls removing teacher • School lion • Kids sorting school bully • School jail • Teacher with long nose • Talking bird • 'Long beard' teacher • Flying class • Big-head kid • Principal with hyenas • Diving practice • A shared hello • Sad kid on first day back • 'Long hair' teacher •

IT'S
KITE-FLYING
TIME
Draw the kites

Remember to practise your stick figures.

RABBIT HOLE

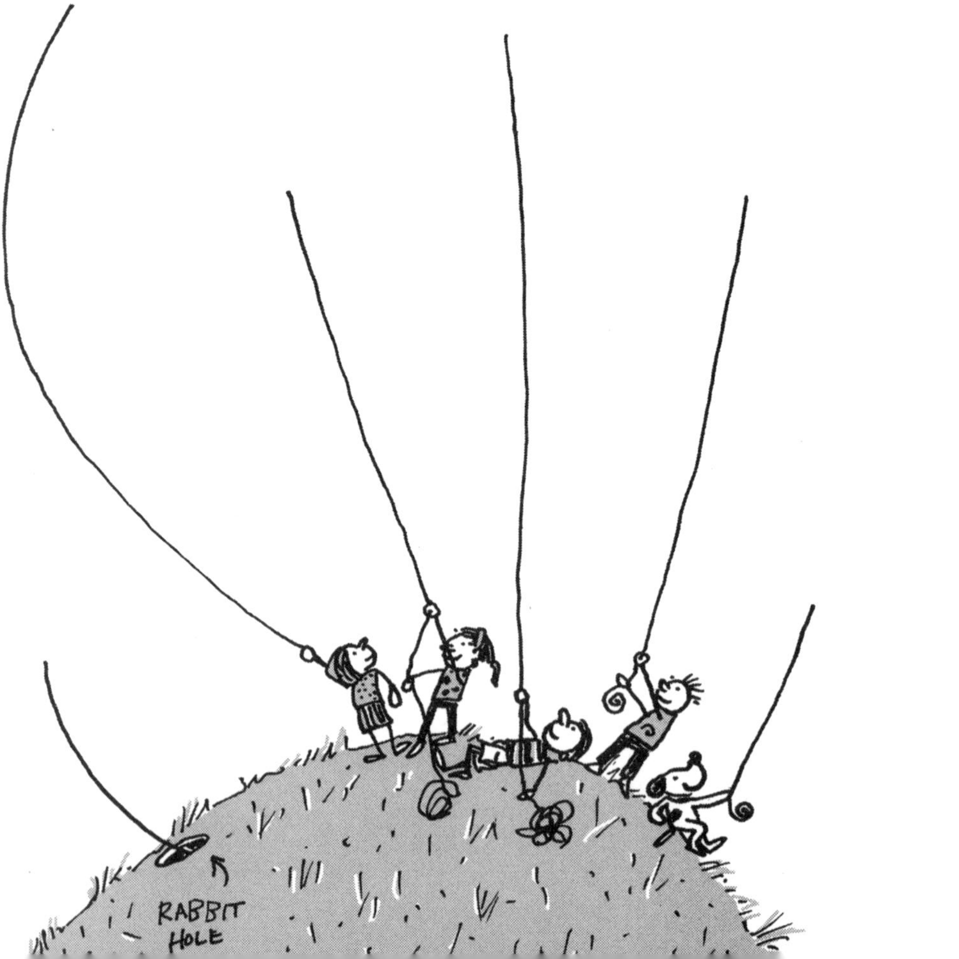

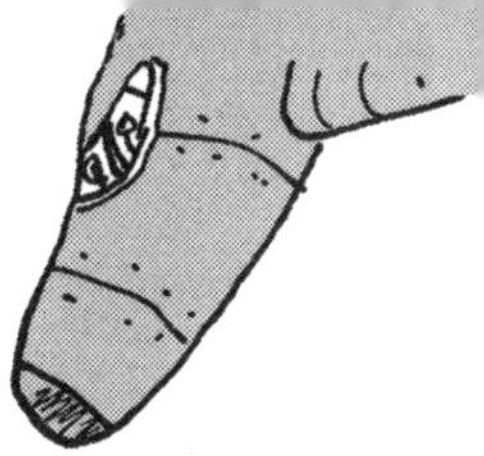

Balloons

And not just planes.

This is perfectly safe... isn't it?

Bathtub

BORED
AT HOME?
LOOK FOR
THINGS WITH
FACES

And not just people.
Or horses.

Door knob

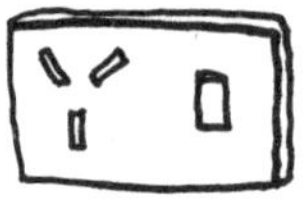
Power point

Inner-city house

You're not a household appliance!
But I am.
me, too.
DRAW
ALL THE HOUSEHOLD
APPLIANCES
WITH STAND-BY
LIGHTS

You suddenly realise it's time to

GO BACK TO SCHOOL!

Draw your expression

WRITE AND DRAW YOUR BEST EXCUSES WHY YOU CAN'T GO BACK TO SCHOOL

I can't go back to school because . . .

I can't go back to school because . . .

I can't go back to school because . . .

I can't go back to school because . . .

WHAT I LOVE / HATE ABOUT BACK TO SCHOOL

DRAW 8 things you left in your schoolbag over the holidays (Oops! Sorry, Mum)

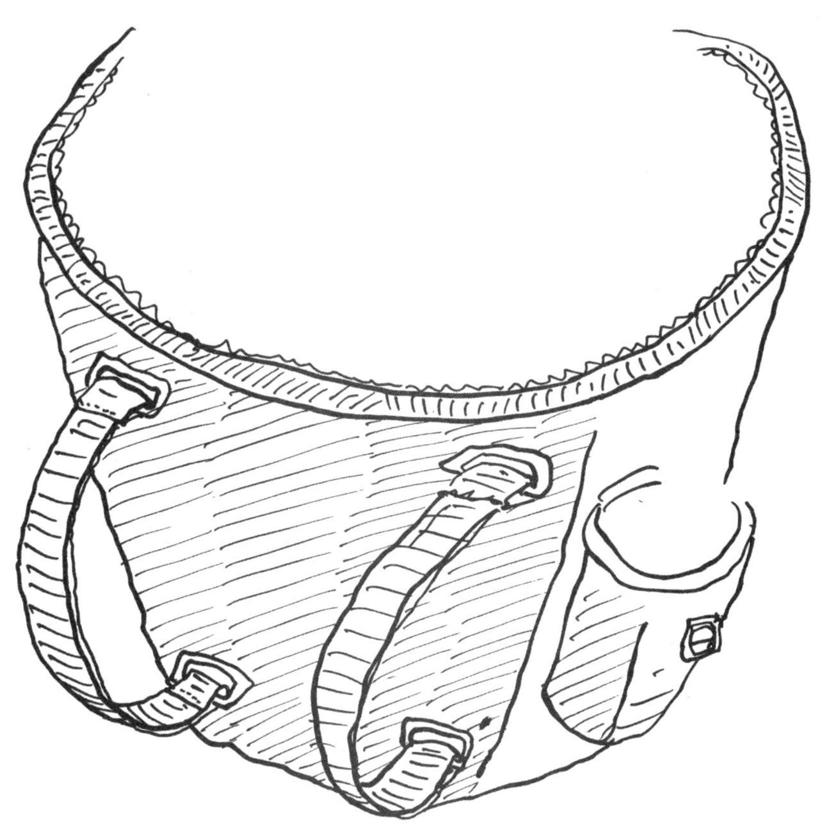

3 FRIENDS YOU CAN'T WAIT TO SEE AGAIN

ME

YOU

3 KIDS YOU NEVER WANT TO SEE AGAIN

ME

YOU

HOW TO TAME THE SCHOOL BULLY
Horse! Let me out of here.
?
UP
Trap him, box him and post him to Venezuela.

FAVOURITE LUNCH TREATS

YOU
DREAM
YOU GET
A CRAZY
HAIRSTYLE

DESIGN YOUR OWN SENSIBLE SCHOOL UNIFORM
umbrella hat
Tails
Best board shorts
Fins for very wet days
Wet suit legs

NOW
DRAW BIRD
AND HORSE
RIDING
THESE THINGS

MOON

NOW DRAW
BIRD AND
HORSE
RIDING TO
SCHOOL

AND NOW
BIRD, HORSE
AND A COW
RIDING

AND BIRD,
HORSE
A COW AND
A TRACTOR

WHAT ABOUT . . .
TRACTOR,
HORSE,
COW,
BIRD

...HORSE,
TRACTOR,
BIRD,
COW...

...COW,
TRACTOR,
BIRD,
HORSE...

...HORSE,
BIRD,
COW,
COW,
COW,
COW...

...COW...

STOP!

YOU HAVE COME TO...

THE END...

THE
END
COW

SO... TAKE OUT
YOUR COLOUR PENCILS
AND DO WHAT I WOULD
LOVE
TO
DO...

COLOUR
ALL THE
PAGES!!

Answer to bird page 181: How many bird's eggs? 12.
Answer to cat page 192: Lots!

. . . and I'll see you at
terrydenton.com.au
for more fun!

A mini book of facts packed with maximum humour!

Don't miss Terry's bestselling tour of the history and science of our planet and universe! Explore the ins and outs of biology, geography, geology and the weather, how life evolved and how it works, and how people use chemistry and the forces of nature to create AMAZING things. There's even a chapter on time! Get ready to laugh and be amazed with Professor Terry Denton.

If you've loved this brilliant bumper book, get your hands on another boredom buster - full of funny, crazy, yucky, weird and downright silly drawings, activities, cartoons, puzzles and games!

Great for holidays, car trips, rainy days, slow times, lunchtimes or ANY TIMES!

Winner of the 2019 NSW Premier's History Awards, Young People's History Prize.

Read the un-put-down-able history of Down Under – unexpected, heroic and sometimes tragic. But never EVER boring.

'Marvellous . . . a great introduction to Australian history.'
THE DAILY TELEGRAPH

' . . . you are in for an irreverent rollicking ride'
MAGPIES MAGAZINE

MORE MARVELLOUS BOOKS FROM YOUR FAVOURITE PROFESSOR OF EVERYTHING!

For anyone who likes their history funny, gruesome, action-packed and thrilling!

Dream astronaut dreams, and celebrate Australia's role in one of humanity's greatest achievements, the moon landing of 1969.

'Vivid and engaging . . .'
BETTER READING